BLOODLINE BOUND

by Sha'Ron Robertson

For every bloodline that carries both darkness and light — may you choose your own path.

"BLOODBLINE BOUND"

By: Sha'Ron Robertson

CHAPTER ONE

Ashes and Shadows

The sky over Willow Creek hung heavy and gray, a bruised color, as if mourning alongside them.

Aya gripped the damp program in her hand, the edges curling under her trembling fingers. Her grandmother's face stared up from the glossy paper, frozen in a black-and-white portrait taken long before Aya was born. A woman of sharp cheekbones and piercing eyes, dressed in her Sunday best, crowned with a tilt of pride.

The funeral crowd was gathered thick under the oak trees, their heads bowed, their clothes dark — deep purples, blacks, blues — as if they could armor themselves against grief.
Someone hummed a hymn, low and throaty, and the sound traveled through the mourners like a ghost moving through a room.

The pastor's words blurred at the edges of Aya's mind. She focused instead on the rituals unfolding around her.
An elder woman, Ms. Delphine, moved gracefully down the rows, offering a pressed

white handkerchief to each mourner.
When she reached Aya, her weathered hand
lingered a beat longer, pressing the cloth into
Aya's palm as if passing more than just fabric
— passing a burden.

Across the field, beyond the tidy rows of
chairs and caskets, Aya caught sight of
someone standing beneath a twisted cypress
tree.

A woman — tall, thin, wrapped in a dark
shawl — her face completely hidden.

No one else seemed to notice her.

The woman didn't move, didn't blink,
just watched.

Aya's chest tightened.

The final prayer was said, the ashes
blessed. Family members took turns dropping
soil into the open grave, the thud of it against
the coffin unnervingly loud in the thick air.

When Aya stepped forward, her body
moved on instinct.
Her fingers let the earth fall, but as she did,
the breeze shifted sharply —
and she heard her name.

"Aya..."

A whisper, unmistakable.

She froze, scanning the crowd. Everyone else was somber, distracted by grief. No one had spoken.

When Aya looked back toward the cypress tree, the woman was gone.

Later, at the gathering, the air was lighter but still strained, the way it always was when death visited a family.

The folding tables inside the community hall sagged under the weight of food: macaroni and cheese, fried chicken, collard greens slick with pot liquor. Comfort food, meant to fill the hollow left behind.

Chrissy plopped onto the bench beside Aya, two heavy plates balanced on her lap.

"Eat," she ordered, nudging a fork into Aya's hand. "Or Miss Rose gon' fuss at you for looking like you 'bout to faint."

Aya forced a smile, but the taste of food turned to ash in her mouth. She pushed the plate aside and stared out the hall's window.

Chrissy leaned in, lowering her voice. "You saw her, didn't you?"

Aya stiffened. "Saw who?"

Chrissy's gaze flicked to the door, as if expecting someone to materialize.
"The woman. Out there. Dressed all wrong for this heat."

Aya's blood ran cold.
"You saw her too?"

Chrissy nodded grimly. "Since the blood moon last month, I been seeing...things. Shadows where they ain't supposed to be. Voices whispering when the wind blow."

Aya's stomach twisted.

Before she could respond, Ms. Delphine approached their table, her cane tapping a slow rhythm on the floor.

She fixed Aya with a stare that felt heavier than the humid air.
"Blood remembers," she said cryptically.
Then she turned and shuffled away, leaving the words hanging in the space between them like smoke.

That night, Aya tossed restlessly in bed, the heat of the day refusing to leave the small house.

Sleep came in fits and starts — until it didn't come at all.

She woke up gasping from a dream she couldn't entirely recall: a crossroads carved into dirt, candles burning low, a voice whispering from all four corners.

In the dream, the woman from the funeral had beckoned to her with a hand as thin as bone, drawing her deeper into the unknown.

Aya pressed her hands to her face, trying to banish the lingering dread.

When she lowered them, she saw it — faint but unmistakable.

A mark.

Burned into the center of her palm: a rough circle surrounded by four smaller dots.

The same symbol she had glimpsed scratched into Grandmother's headstone.

[End of Chapter 1.]

CHAPTER TWO

Old Warnings

Morning in Willow Creek came slow and heavy.

Aya sat at the edge of her bed, staring at the faint mark on her palm. She rubbed at it furiously, but it wouldn't fade.
It wasn't just a dream. It wasn't her imagination.

It was real.

Downstairs, she could hear her mother moving around the kitchen, the clink of a coffee pot and the scrape of a chair against the old linoleum floor. Normal sounds. Everyday life.

But nothing about today felt normal.

Aya dressed quickly — jeans, a worn T-shirt, sneakers — clothes she could move in if she had to.

When she came downstairs, her mother, Denise, glanced up from her coffee. Her eyes were puffy from crying, but her mouth was set in a familiar tight line. The face of a

woman who survived by pretending
everything was fine until it actually was.

"You feeling alright, baby?" Denise
asked, her voice rough around the edges.

Aya hesitated. Should she tell her? Show
her the mark?

But some instinct — a deep, gut feeling
— said no.
Not yet.

"I'm fine," she lied. "Just tired."

Her mother nodded slowly, not pushing.
"Well, don't let grief pull you under. Your
grandma wouldn't want that."

Aya mumbled something in return,
grabbing a biscuit from the counter and
heading toward the door.

"Hey," Denise called after her, making
her pause. "Be careful out there today."

Aya turned. "Why? Something happen?"

Her mother hesitated just a second too
long. "Storm's coming," she said finally. "You
know how the trees get — dropping
branches, blocking roads."

But Aya caught the flicker of something else in her mother's face — something like fear.

She didn't ask. She just nodded and left.

Outside, the sun glared weakly through a sky thick with clouds. The air felt charged, like static before a lightning strike.

Aya found Chrissy waiting for her at the edge of the cemetery, sitting on the low stone wall that bordered the graves.

Chrissy was dressed like she was headed to battle — boots, cargo pants, a black tank top. Her hair was pulled back in tight braids, exposing the stern set of her jaw.

"You ready?" Chrissy asked, tossing a small backpack to her.

"For what?"

Chrissy's lips twitched into something that wasn't quite a smile. "To figure out what the hell is going on."

Aya caught the bag. It clinked with something metallic. She unzipped it and found a flashlight, some rope, and a thick leather-bound book that looked ancient.

"Where did you get this?" Aya asked, thumbing through brittle pages covered in hand-written symbols.

"Found it in my grandma's attic last night," Chrissy said. "She used to say our family had roots. Deep ones. Told me to stay away from the woods by the old mill... said things lived there that remembered the old blood."

Aya frowned. "Old blood?"

Chrissy shrugged. "Old magic. Old debts."

The words sent a chill down Aya's spine. She thought of the woman under the cypress tree, of the mark now burned into her skin.

"Look," Chrissy said, suddenly serious. "I don't know exactly what's going on. But you and me — we're in it now. Whether we want to be or not."

Aya exhaled slowly. "Where do we start?"

Chrissy stood, slinging her own bag over one shoulder. "At the place no one talks about. The old crossroads behind Hallow's Field."

Aya's heart skipped a beat. That was the place from her dream.
The crossroads.

Maybe the answers — or at least some of them — were waiting for them there.

They made their way through town, skirting around nosy neighbors and weaving through back alleys. People were acting strange today — whispering behind hands, locking doors earlier than usual, crossing themselves when they saw Aya and Chrissy pass.

It was like the whole town knew something was brewing.

The road to Hallow's Field was half-forgotten, overgrown with weeds and framed by ancient trees. Birds fell silent when they passed. Even the bugs seemed to stay away.

As they approached the field, Chrissy pulled Aya to a stop.

"You sure about this?" she asked, her voice low.

"No," Aya admitted.

But she moved forward anyway.

At the far edge of the field, hidden behind tall grass and thistles, they found it: a crossroads.
Four dirt paths meeting at a barren center.
In the very middle sat a weathered wooden post, leaning at a crooked angle, with strips of cloth and rusted trinkets tied around it.

The air smelled like copper and smoke.

Aya stepped closer, her palm burning hotter with every footstep.

As she reached out to touch the post, the ground beneath her feet shifted.

A crack split the earth — just a hairline at first, then wider, revealing something glinting deep inside the dirt.

A box.

Chrissy dropped to her knees, brushing soil aside with frantic hands.

Together, they unearthed it: a small, iron-bound box, etched with symbols that matched the ones in Chrissy's attic book.

Aya hesitated — her instincts screaming don't open it — but something older, deeper, louder inside her said you must.

With a trembling hand, she unlatched the box.

Inside was a bundle wrapped in faded red cloth. When Aya peeled it back, she found…

A bone.

Small, delicate, not animal.

Human.

And tucked beneath it, a folded piece of parchment, yellowed and crumbling.

The writing was in a language Aya couldn't read — but the final line was scrawled in English, jagged and hurried.

It said:

"Blood binds. Blood calls. Blood claims."

Aya swallowed hard.

Whatever this was — whatever her grandmother had tried to protect them from — it wasn't finished.

It was just beginning.

[End of Chapter 2.]

CHAPTER THREE

Whispers Beneath the Soil

The world seemed to tilt as Aya and Chrissy stared at the contents of the iron box.

For a moment, neither of them moved. The only sound was the shallow whisper of the wind threading through the crossroads.

Aya's heart hammered in her ears.

"Blood binds. Blood calls. Blood claims."

She couldn't stop staring at the bone resting in the cloth. It was no bigger than her finger, but something about it thrummed with power — or maybe it was a warning.

Chrissy finally broke the silence.

"We should put it back," she said, voice tight. "We shouldn't have touched it."

Aya wanted to agree, but she couldn't move her legs. It was like her body was tethered to the spot, as if invisible roots were winding up her ankles, holding her there.

"The dream," Aya whispered. "It led me here."

Chrissy frowned. "Dream?"

Aya told her — about the woman in the cypress, about the words she spoke, about the mark that still pulsed faintly on her palm. As she spoke, Chrissy's expression grew darker.

"You should have told me," Chrissy said, glancing nervously around the deserted field. "That sounds like a summoning."

"A what?"

Chrissy opened her bag and yanked out the old book. She flipped through the brittle pages with shaking fingers until she found a sketch — a woman tied to a tree, black vines wrapped around her body, mouth open in silent scream.

"A binding spell," Chrissy said, tapping the drawing. "Someone called you to it. Woke it up."

Aya shivered. "Why me?"

Before Chrissy could answer, the earth beneath their feet trembled — a subtle vibration at first, then stronger.

From the woods beyond the crossroads, a low murmur rose — voices, layered and indistinct.

Chrissy snapped the book shut. "We need to move. Now."

They stuffed the box back into the hole, kicking dirt over it. As they turned to leave, Aya caught a flash of movement at the tree line: dark shapes, half-seen, slipping between the trunks.

Watching.

Waiting.

Her skin crawled with the certainty that the things in the woods were not human.

They ran — stumbling through the tall grass, feet slipping in the wet soil — and didn't stop until they reached the gravel road leading back toward town.

Only then did they dare to look back.

Nothing. Just empty fields and the rustle of the trees.

But Aya knew it wasn't over. Whatever they had disturbed — whatever blood-debt had been buried — it had tasted air again.

And it wanted more.

That night, Aya couldn't sleep.

The wind howled outside her window, rattling the panes like skeletal fingers tapping to be let in.

She lay in bed, staring at the ceiling, the events of the day replaying in her mind on a sickening loop.

The bone.
The parchment.
The way the earth had cracked open like a living thing.

A sudden noise snapped her head up — a scratching sound, faint but steady, coming from her closet.

At first, she told herself it was just the house settling. Old houses made noise all the time.

But then she heard it again — louder — the distinct sound of fingernails dragging across wood.

Her throat tightened.

"Aya..." a voice hissed from the darkness.

It wasn't her mother's voice. It wasn't Chrissy's.

It was the voice from her dream.

Aya bolted upright. She grabbed the baseball bat she kept under her bed — a relic from her brief middle-school softball phase — and crept toward the closet.

The scratching stopped.

Her heart thudded painfully against her ribs.

She raised the bat high and yanked the closet door open—

Nothing.

Just her clothes, a pair of worn shoes, a dusty box of old notebooks.

But the smell hit her then — coppery, like blood, thick enough to make her gag.

Aya stumbled back, slamming the door shut and bracing her back against it, her chest heaving.

Across the room, on her mirror, a single word had appeared, scrawled in something dark and wet:

"Bound."

Aya squeezed her eyes shut.

When she opened them again, the word was still there.

There was no denying it anymore: she was caught in something ancient and hungry, something that had slept beneath Willow Creek's pretty surface for centuries.

And now it was awake.

[End of Chapter 3.]

CHAPTER FOUR

Echoes of the Past

The next morning, Aya felt like a hollow version of herself.

She barely touched her breakfast, barely heard her mother's concerned questions. Her mind replayed the events of the night — the whisper, the word written across the mirror.

Bound.

She hadn't told her mother. How could she? How do you explain to someone who believes in Sunday services and polite smiles that something ancient had slipped into your life and slammed the door behind it?

By the time she met up with Chrissy outside the library, the sun was high, but Aya still shivered like she was walking through a winter storm.

"You look like hell," Chrissy said bluntly.

"I didn't sleep," Aya muttered.

Chrissy held the library door open. "Neither did I."

The Willow Creek Library was an old stone building that smelled of dust, old wood, and secrets. It had been there since the late 1800s, rebuilt after a mysterious fire in 1924 that no one in town seemed eager to talk about.

They headed for the local history section, tucked away in a corner rarely visited by anyone under the age of seventy. Chrissy dropped her heavy bag onto a table and pulled out the old book again, along with a couple of other volumes she'd snagged from her grandfather's attic.

"We need answers," Chrissy said. "Before it gets worse."

Aya sat heavily in the chair and rubbed her temples. "What even are we looking for?"

Chrissy flipped a page, revealing a hand-drawn map of Willow Creek — but it was different. Roads that no longer existed. Names of places forgotten.

"There," Chrissy said, jabbing her finger at a marked 'X' on the map — right where the crossroads stood now.

Aya leaned in. "It used to be a plantation?"

Chrissy nodded grimly. "The Blackwell Plantation. Owned by the Blackwell family — real bastards by the sound of it. They ran the whole area, used slave labor even after emancipation. When the town tried to run them out, they retaliated."

Aya swallowed thickly. "Retaliated how?"

Chrissy flipped the page.

There, in an old newspaper clipping, was the headline:

Mass Disappearance at Blackwell Plantation — Entire Village Vanishes Overnight

The article was faded and yellowed, but the basics were clear: dozens of people — freed slaves, poor farmers, anyone who had dared to oppose the Blackwells — had vanished without a trace. Their homes were found abandoned, meals half-eaten, candles still burning.

And at the center of it all — the Blackwell family had disappeared too. Only one body had ever been found.

The matriarch.
Eleanor Blackwell.

Hanged from the ancient cypress tree at the crossroads, with strange symbols carved into her skin.

Aya recoiled from the page.

"That's who you saw in your dream," Chrissy whispered. "The woman in the tree."

Aya's stomach turned. "But why me?"

Chrissy hesitated. Then, from her bag, she pulled out a family tree — one she'd painstakingly drawn from records she'd found in the church's dusty archive.

At the bottom, under a name Aya recognized as one of her great-grandmothers, was a connection she hadn't known existed.

"You're related to them," Chrissy said, voice barely above a whisper. "Through your mother's side. You're a descendant."

The room seemed to spin around Aya.

"My family...?" she croaked.

Chrissy nodded. "Not the Blackwells. The ones who fought them. You come from the line that tried to stop the blood magic."

Aya's mind reeled.

Her mother, so proper and put-together, always talking about respectability and education — had she known? Had someone tried to keep it hidden to protect her?

It didn't matter.
The bloodline remembered, even if she didn't.

And now, so did the darkness.

Later that afternoon, they stood again at the crossroads.

The earth looked untouched, but Aya could feel it — the tension, like the ground itself was breathing slow and deep beneath their feet.

Chrissy pulled out a small glass jar filled with salt and something that smelled like sage.

"Protection spell," she explained. "Basic stuff. It won't hold forever, but maybe it'll buy us time."

As Chrissy sprinkled the mixture in a careful circle around the crossroads, Aya placed her palm against the trunk of the cypress tree.

The mark from her dream flared painfully, and in a rush of vision she saw:

Chains buried beneath the soil.

Faces twisted in terror.

Blood soaking into the roots.

And at the center of it all, Eleanor Blackwell — her face serene, her eyes burning with unnatural light.

Aya jerked back with a gasp.

"The soil's cursed," she said. "It's not just the tree. It's everything. It's...waiting."

Chrissy looked around uneasily. "Waiting for what?"

Aya didn't know. But deep in her bones, she felt the answer — a truth too terrifying to say aloud:

It was waiting for her.

[End of Chapter 4.]

CHAPTER FIVE

Warnings in the Wind

The wind picked up as Aya and Chrissy stepped away from the crossroads, swirling dust and dead leaves around them like a living thing. The salt ring Chrissy had painstakingly laid down scattered into the air within seconds — as if some unseen force rejected their protection.

Chrissy cursed under her breath. "That's not supposed to happen."

Aya didn't answer. Her skin prickled with unease, every hair on her arms standing on end.
Something was changing. The ground felt thinner beneath her feet, as if she were standing on cracked ice, and something old and patient lurked underneath, waiting for the final break.

They hurried back into town, but the feeling followed them — like invisible fingers brushing the back of Aya's neck.

By the time they reached Chrissy's car, the sky had darkened unnaturally, clouds heavy and low. Not a single bird chirped. No squirrels rustled in the trees. The world held its breath.

Chrissy fumbled with her keys. "We need to find out exactly what we're up against. This isn't just some old haunting."

"No," Aya said, climbing into the passenger seat. "It's something worse."

At Chrissy's house, they barricaded themselves in her attic room — the one crammed full of thrift-store finds, half-read books, and strange artifacts she'd collected over the years.

Chrissy dumped everything onto the floor: dusty spellbooks, battered journals, yellowed maps, and tattered family records.

Aya sank into a beanbag chair, feeling exhausted and wired all at once.

"Start from the beginning," she said. "What do you know about blood magic?"

Chrissy rifled through a leather-bound book, stopping at a page that made her frown. "It's old magic," she said slowly. "Older than Christianity. It's rooted in life itself — blood being the purest symbol of life. Some used it for healing. Others... not so much."

She traced a finger down the page.

"When the Blackwells got pushed out of power, they turned to blood rituals to keep what little influence they had. Sacrifices. Binding spells. Even death curses."

Aya swallowed. "And the people who disappeared...?"

Chrissy closed the book with a heavy thud. "They were used. Their life forces fed into the land. The Blackwells boundthe souls to this place, locking them into an endless loop of suffering."

Aya felt sick.

"But why come after me now?" she whispered.

Chrissy leaned forward, voice low. "Because you're the key. Your blood can undo what they did... or finish what they started."

The attic light flickered, and for a moment, Aya swore she saw a shadow standing behind Chrissy — tall, thin, wrong.

She bolted upright. "Did you see that?"

Chrissy whipped around, but the corner was empty.

"You're seeing into the Other Place," Chrissy said, voice grim. "The barrier's wearing thin."

Aya's breath came in shallow gasps. "What do we do?"

Chrissy grabbed her hand, grounding her. "We fight. We research. We find the right counter-spell."

Aya nodded — but deep down, fear gnawed at her.

Because somewhere out there, Eleanor Blackwell — or whatever was left of her — was waking up.

And she wanted Aya.

Later that night, Aya couldn't sleep.

She lay on Chrissy's floor, staring at the ceiling while the house groaned and shifted around her.
Somewhere downstairs, the old grandfather clock ticked too slowly, each second stretching into minutes.

When she finally dozed off, the nightmares came:

She walked endless fields of blood-red grass.
In the distance, the cypress tree loomed against a sky of swirling ash.
Voices cried out from the ground beneath her feet, hands clawing up from the soil, grabbing her ankles.

Then — a woman stepped out from the shadows.

Eleanor Blackwell.

Her face was cracked porcelain, her smile sharp as broken glass.

"You cannot run, child," she whispered. "It's in your blood. In your bones. You belong to us."

Aya woke with a strangled gasp, cold sweat clinging to her skin.

The attic was silent — except for a faint scratching at the window.

She turned her head, heart hammering.

Pressed against the glass, grinning wide, was a pale, corpse-thin face — with eyes black as pitch.

[End of Chapter 5.]

CHAPTER SIX

Scratches in the Night

Aya froze.

For a heartbeat, she couldn't move, couldn't breathe. Her brain struggled to make sense of what she was seeing — the gaunt face, the empty black eyes, the way it smiled too wide, too sharp.

Then the scratching started again.

A single, skeletal finger dragging slowly down the glass.

Scrrraaaaape.

Aya scrambled backward, tripping over Chrissy's discarded books and crashing into the nightstand. The lamp toppled, plunging the room into near darkness.

Chrissy jerked awake at the noise, blinking groggily. "Aya? What the hell?"

Aya pointed with a shaking hand. "Window—"

Chrissy whipped around just in time to see the face melt into shadow, leaving behind only a faint smear on the glass.

Without hesitation, Chrissy grabbed a mason jar from her shelf and shook out a handful of dried herbs, muttering under her breath in a language Aya didn't recognize. She scattered the herbs across the window sill, tracing a sigil with her finger.

The scratching stopped.

The oppressive weight lifted — slightly.

Chrissy locked the window and pulled the curtains tight. "It can't come in unless you invite it."

Aya hugged herself tightly. "What was that?"

Chrissy's face was pale. "A harbinger. A messenger of death. It's warning you: if you keep digging, they'll come for you."

Aya swallowed hard. "I'm already in it. We both are."

Chrissy nodded grimly. "Then we need to move faster."

The next morning, they hit the town library.

It was a crumbling relic from the 1800s, all towering shelves and dusty chandeliers, tucked between two abandoned storefronts. Nobody paid them much attention — small towns had a way of ignoring things they didn't want to see.

They pored over historical records, property maps, town meeting notes — anything that could hint at the Blackwell family's true history.

Hours passed.

Books piled up around them like little fortresses.

And then Aya found it.

An old newspaper clipping, buried in a crumbling leather folder:

"Mysterious Disappearances at Blackwell Plantation: Locals Suspect Foul Play — Authorities Remain Silent."
June 5th, 1868.

There was a grainy photo of the plantation house — looking almost identical to how it stood now — and standing on the front steps was a woman in a dark dress, a parasol at her side.

Aya felt the blood drain from her face.

It was her.

Eleanor Blackwell.

The same woman from her nightmare.

Chrissy leaned over, reading aloud: "'Several families reported missing after visiting the Blackwell estate. Survivors claim to hear singing in the fields and to see ghostly figures walking the plantation grounds at night. Blackwell heirs deny involvement.'"

She looked up, eyes wide. "They were hunting people."

Aya clutched the folder. "We need to see that house."

Chrissy hesitated. "You sure?"

"No," Aya said honestly. "But if we're going to end this... we have to."

That night, they stood at the edge of the Blackwell property.

The plantation house loomed ahead, shrouded in mist. Its once-white columns were cracked and blackened, the roof sagging like a dying animal. No light shone from within, but the windows watched them like hollow eyes.

The air tasted of ash and salt.

Aya's fingers trembled around the iron key they had found hidden in the library records — a key said to unlock the Blackwell family vault.

"We go in," Chrissy said, voice tight. "We find whatever's tying her spirit here. We end it."

Aya nodded.

And together, they crossed the threshold.

The door creaked open with a sound like a dying scream.

Inside, the house exhaled — a long, cold breath that smelled of blood and old sorrow.

And somewhere deep within the darkness, something woke up.

Waiting for them.

[End of Chapter 6.]

CHAPTER SEVEN

The House that Remembers

The moment Aya and Chrissy stepped inside, the door slammed shut behind them.

Aya spun around, heart racing, but the knob wouldn't budge. It was like the house had swallowed them whole.

"Stay close," Chrissy whispered, pulling a small sachet of herbs from her pocket. "It's alive. It remembers."

The foyer stretched endlessly before them, lit only by the pale moonlight seeping through the cracked windows. Portraits of grim-faced ancestors lined the walls, their painted eyes seeming to track the girls' every move.

Aya shivered. "Which way?"

Chrissy consulted the torn blueprints they'd found at the library. "Vault's supposed to be in the basement."

Aya grimaced. Of course it was.

They started forward, each step heavy and reluctant. The floorboards groaned under their weight, some giving slightly as if something beneath them shifted in response.

In the dining hall, the long mahogany table was still set for a feast that never happened — plates of dusty porcelain, silverware tarnished black. Faded napkins were folded into elegant swans, untouched by time.

Chrissy paused, staring at a place setting marked with a nameplate:

"AYA BLACKWELL"

Aya's mouth went dry.
"No... no, that can't be—"

Before Chrissy could answer, the chandelier above them shuddered violently. Dust rained down. Somewhere deeper in the house, a low, guttural voice began to chant — a dirge in a language Aya didn't recognize.

They ran.

Through a hallway where the wallpaper peeled like shedding skin.
Past doors that thudded and rattled on their hinges.
Down a grand staircase where bloody handprints smeared the banister.

The air grew colder with every step.

At the base of the stairs, they found the basement door — a thick slab of wood bound with iron.

Aya hesitated. "Are we really doing this?"

Chrissy squeezed her hand. "If we don't... this never ends."

Together, they unlocked the door.

The basement was pitch-black.

As they descended, the temperature dropped sharply, each breath misting in the air. Their flashlights cut narrow tunnels of light through the suffocating darkness, revealing glimpses of broken furniture, shattered glass, old trunks.

Aya's beam landed on a large iron vault embedded into the stone wall.

"That's it," she whispered.

Chrissy approached it cautiously, the key trembling in her hand.

Just as she inserted it—

A shriek ripped through the basement, high and inhuman.

The air exploded with a blast of icy wind, slamming them against the walls.

From the shadows, figures emerged — the lost souls of the plantation, their eyes hollow, their mouths sewn shut with black thread.

One by one, they reached for Aya.

Above them, the house began to crumble.

Plaster rained down. Beams cracked. The very foundation shook with rage.

Chrissy screamed over the din, "OPEN IT, AYA! NOW!"

Aya staggered toward the vault, her body heavy as if invisible hands tried to drag her down. She shoved the key into the lock, twisting with all her strength.

The vault door groaned... then swung open.

Inside was a small, velvet-lined box.

With trembling fingers, Aya lifted the lid.

Inside, resting atop faded red velvet, was a bundle of yellowed papers — contracts.

Contracts signed in blood.
Binding generations of Blackwell descendants
to Eleanor's curse.

A whispered voice filled her mind,
seductive and cold:
"Join us. Fulfill the bond."

Aya's vision swam. She could see flashes
of herself standing beside Eleanor, dressed in
black, laughing in the fields of the dead.

"No," she whispered.

She turned — and set the papers on fire.

The flames roared to life, blue and
hungry, swallowing the contracts whole. The
spirits shrieked in agony, their forms flickering
and dissolving into ash.

The house screamed with them.

Walls split open. Ceilings collapsed.
Smoke billowed upward in thick, choking
waves.

Chrissy grabbed Aya's hand, dragging her
toward the stairs. "GO!"

They raced through the crumbling house,
dodging falling debris, the fire chasing at their

heels. The portraits melted from the walls, the floor buckled underfoot.

Finally, they burst through the front door into the cool night air just as the entire plantation behind them caved in with a thunderous roar.

Aya collapsed onto the grass, coughing, her heart pounding.

It was over.

Or so she thought.

From the edge of the woods, hidden in the mist, a woman watched them.

Eleanor Blackwell.

Smiling.

Waiting.

[End of Chapter 7.]

CHAPTER EIGHT

The Reckoning

The night after the plantation collapsed, the rain had stopped—but not the storm that raged within Aya's heart. The cool, damp air of early morning carried a stillness that was almost eerie, as if the world itself were holding its breath after the violence of the previous hours.

Aya and Chrissy sat side by side on the overgrown front steps of what once was the Blackwell estate. The ruin lay scattered before them like broken memories—twisted beams, splintered wood, and ash drifting in the pale light. The devastation was absolute, yet it did nothing to ease the gnawing dread that had settled deep in Aya's bones.

"Do you think it's over?" Chrissy whispered, her voice trembling as she surveyed the smoldering remains. Her eyes darted to the dark line of the treeline, where, even in the dawn, shapes seemed to move just beyond sight.

Aya's gaze was fixed on a solitary figure emerging from the shadows at the edge of the ruin—the face of Eleanor Blackwell, unmistakable even in death. Her eyes burned with a sorrowful fire, and her smile was somehow both mocking and mournful. The sight made Aya's pulse spike.

"It's not over," Aya murmured. "She's still here…watching."

The apparition drifted forward, silent but powerful—a spectral reminder that the curse still clung tightly to the land and its bloodline. The wind picked up, rustling the charred leaves and carrying with it a low, mournful cadence as if the land itself were singing a dirge.

Aya clenched her fist around the battered relic that still lay hidden within her jacket. Its glow had dimmed to a faint ember, but its power was unmistakable—a constant reminder of the inheritance she'd been forced to claim. In that moment, the weight of her bloodline felt heavier than ever.

Chrissy's eyes met Aya's. "We broke the contracts," she said softly, "but the curse…it's deeper than just a set of bindings on paper. It's woven into the very soil. The ancestors … they still suffer."

Aya looked back to the ghostly figure of Eleanor. "She's here, calling us to account,"

Aya replied, voice tight with both defiance and fear. "Maybe this is our final reckoning."

As the first rays of the sun pushed through the remnants of clouds, the air shimmered with an otherworldly quality. A low, almost imperceptible hum filled the space—a vibration that rose from the earth beneath their feet. It was as though every stone, every splintered beam, and every charred remnant was alive with whispered voices of the past.

A sudden, intense gust of wind howled past them, and the figure of Eleanor drew closer. Now, the spirit's face was clearer—a face not warped by rage but lined with bitter regret. The spectral figure extended a translucent hand toward Aya, as if pleading for something lost.

Aya's breath caught in her throat. "What do you want?" she called out, her voice echoing in the sudden stillness. The figure's eyes locked with hers, and for a moment, Aya felt as if she were peering into a mirror of her own soul—haunted, conflicted, and desperately yearning for release.

The voice of Eleanor, soft yet resonant, finally broke the silence. "Your blood... it bears the promise of redemption and destruction. The pact was sealed long ago. Now, the balance must be restored. You alone can choose which fate our line will bear."

Around them, the ground pulsed as if in reply. Old oak trees shuddered, and the scent of wet earth and decayed leaves mixed with something metallic—blood, perhaps. The supernatural energy was almost palpable, a reminder that the past could never be fully buried.

Chrissy stepped forward, her tone a mix of urgency and compassion. "Aya, listen to her. This isn't just a curse—it's a choice. Our ancestors fought, we fought. If we let the darkness consume us, nothing is left. But if we embrace the light... if we find our own way to heal, maybe the old wounds can close."

Aya's thoughts churned as conflicting emotions battled inside her. In her mind, images of generations lost, of endless sacrifices made in vain, warred with visions of hope—a future where the bloodline would be free from the chains of ancient sins. The relic in her pocket pulsed slowly, as if urging her on.

For what felt like an eternity, Aya stood at the precipice of decision. The spectral Eleanor lingered, an embodiment of the past's grief and unspoken promises. Finally, Aya's voice, low and steady, broke the quiet.

"I choose... to end this cycle," she declared. "Not by clinging to the bitterness of the past, but by forging a new path for those who come after me. I choose freedom—for our souls, for our family, for all who have suffered."

At her words, the relic in her jacket flared to life—a brilliant, cleansing light that spread outward from Aya like a pulse, rippling through the earth, through the ruin, through the very air. The ground trembled, and the oppressive weight of centuries seemed to lift, replaced by a tentative hope.

Eleanor's apparition softened, her eyes welling with something that resembled gratitude. "Then may the ancestors find peace," the spirit intoned, before slowly dissolving into glittering motes that danced on the morning breeze.

For a few long, silent moments, Aya and Chrissy remained on the broken steps, absorbing the magnitude of what had just transpired. The house and the cursed ground, though scarred, now felt... quieter. Lighter. As if a long-held burden was finally being lifted.

Chrissy reached over, taking Aya's hand. "Do you feel it?" she asked. "The heaviness… it's easing."

Aya squeezed Chrissy's hand tightly. "I think we did it, Chrissy. I think we chose our destiny."

But even as the first hopeful birds began to sing and the haze of twilight dispersed, a lingering uncertainty hovered in Aya's mind. The relic lay dormant now—a simple, unremarkable stone in its diminished form— but she knew that darkness and light, hope and despair, would always coexist. The price of freedom was never truly paid in full.

As they slowly walked away from the ruin, Aya glanced back one last time. In the distance, barely visible among the trees, a solitary figure watched them: the ghost of Eleanor Blackwell, her expression unreadable, her fate still intertwined with the land.

Aya whispered, "May we all find our peace."

And with that, the ancestral storm subsided—at least for now.

[End of Chapter 8.]

CHAPTER NINE

Echoes through the Hollow

The town of Millers Hollow had always been a place where secrets whispered louder than the wind, but after the Blackwell plantation burned, the whispers turned into shouts.

Aya and Chrissy returned to the town square days later, feeling like strangers in a place that once barely noticed them. The old men who gathered outside the bait shop paused their conversations when the girls passed. Mothers pulled their children closer. Even the familiar chime of the diner bell seemed sharp, suspicious.

Chrissy shifted uncomfortably as they made their way down Main Street. "They're scared of us," she muttered.

Aya nodded grimly. "They should be."

At the edge of the square, a makeshift memorial had been set up—candles, flowers, and hand-written notes surrounding a black-and-white photograph of the plantation's ruins. At its center was a sign, painted in bold red strokes:

NEVER FORGET. NEVER
FORGIVE.

Aya stared at the sign, her jaw tightening.
She knew the message wasn't just about the
tragedy—it was a warning. The town wasn't
mourning the loss of a cursed estate. They
were mourning the fall of the old powers that
had silently controlled Millers Hollow for
generations.

"Look," Chrissy whispered, nodding
toward the courthouse steps.

A group had gathered there—Sheriff
Barnes, the mayor, a few prominent families
whose bloodlines traced back centuries. Their
faces were a mix of fear, anger, and something
more dangerous: desperation.

Sheriff Barnes stepped forward, adjusting
his worn hat. His voice carried over the
murmuring crowd. "We will be holding an
inquiry into the events that took place at the
Blackwell estate. This town was built on
respect—for history, for tradition. And we
will get answers."

Aya felt the relic in her pocket throb
faintly, a warning.

Chrissy grabbed her arm. "They're looking for someone to blame. They're going to come after us."

Aya's eyes never left Barnes as he scanned the crowd, his gaze lingering on her a moment too long.

"Let them come," Aya whispered fiercely. "I'm not running anymore."

That night, they met with Mrs. Holloway in the back of her bookstore—the only adult in town who had always believed in the deeper truths behind Millers Hollow's polished facade.

Mrs. Holloway, a spry woman with silver hair and fierce green eyes, lit a series of heavy candles around the cramped office. The smell of old books and wax filled the room.

"You girls stirred up something ancient," she said, setting a thick leather-bound book on the table. "The Blackwells weren't just landowners. They were gatekeepers. Their bloodline maintained an ancient barrier, one stitched together by sacrifice and... darker means."

Aya leaned in. "A barrier against what?"

Mrs. Holloway tapped the book. "Against what's beneath Millers Hollow. The plantation wasn't just cursed—it was a seal."

Chrissy paled. "We broke it."

Mrs. Holloway nodded grimly. "You weakened it. Freed the souls enslaved by the Blackwells, yes—but now... other things may be stirring. Things that were never meant to walk freely."

A heavy silence fell over the room.

Aya straightened. "Then we'll fix it."

Mrs. Holloway's eyes softened. "Child, it may not be that simple. Blood opened the door. Blood might be the only thing that can close it."

Aya's stomach turned. She had fought so hard to escape the legacy forced upon her—could she now sacrifice even more to protect the town that despised her?

Mrs. Holloway pushed the book toward them. "You'll need allies. Knowledge. Strength you haven't yet tapped. And maybe," she added gently, "forgiveness—for yourselves, and for the ones who came before you."

The candles flickered violently, as if the very walls of the bookstore trembled at the words spoken.

Outside, the wind howled through the streets of Millers Hollow, carrying with it an ancient hunger newly awakened.

The reckoning had begun. But the true battle was still to come.

And Aya knew she would have to face it head-on—or risk losing not just her bloodline's future, but the soul of Millers Hollow itself.

[End of Chapter 9.]

CHAPTER TEN

The Gathering Storm

The old bookstore was a sanctuary, but it could only shield them for so long.

The town was shifting around them. The winds were sharper, colder. Stray animals disappeared. Birds flew in disjointed, frantic patterns. People whispered in doorways and glanced nervously over their shoulders.

The Hollow was alive—and it was angry.

Mrs. Holloway leaned over the thick tome spread across the table, her fingers tracing the crumbling ink of a map nearly two centuries old.

"This," she said, tapping a spot marked with an ancient symbol, "is the Hollow's heart."

Aya leaned closer. The map showed a hidden valley just beyond the woods, a place no one talked about anymore, a place even the oldest maps blurred and avoided. It was marked simply: Sanctum of the Bound.

Chrissy frowned. "Sanctum? Like... a church?"

Mrs. Holloway shook her head grimly. "No. A prison."

Aya's chest tightened. The echoes of the dreams she had been having—dark woods, red skies, voices speaking in tongues she didn't understand—all pointed to this. Whatever had been sealed, whatever the Blackwells had kept chained, was housed there.

And now it stirred.

"We have to get there before it fully wakes up," Aya said, voice steady despite the fear gnawing at her gut.

"But how do we even find it?" Chrissy asked. "It's not like we can just Google 'ancient supernatural prison' and get directions."

Mrs. Holloway smiled faintly and slid a faded compass across the table. Its needle spun wildly before slowing, pointing steadily to the northwest.

"It's drawn to blood," Mrs. Holloway said softly. "Your blood."

Aya hesitated before taking the compass. The metal was strangely warm, almost pulsing.

It was a direct link to the force she was bound to, whether she liked it or not.

They gathered supplies—salt, old iron nails, protective charms—and prepared for the trek at dawn. Mrs. Holloway warned them of the signs to watch for: twisted trees, sudden silences, unnatural fog.

"Stay together," she warned, gripping Aya's hand with surprising strength. "The Hollow feeds on fear and division. It will try to turn you against each other."

Aya promised they would stay strong. But deep down, a whisper of doubt took root.

When the sun cracked the horizon, muted and blood-orange, they set out.

The woods grew thicker the deeper they went, the air turning dense, like breathing through wet cloth. Twigs snapped underfoot. Shadows seemed to lean toward them.

After an hour, Chrissy stopped, her face pale. "Did you hear that?"

Aya froze, heart pounding. At first, there was nothing. Then—faint, like a memory— the sound of laughter. Children's laughter.

Chrissy clutched Aya's arm. "There's nobody here, Aya."

Aya tightened her grip on the compass. The needle still pointed forward, unerring.

"We're close," she said.

The laughter grew louder. Then turned into crying. Then into screaming.

They pushed on, fighting every instinct to turn back. The trees twisted unnaturally above them, branches forming crude shapes—faces, hands, mouths frozen mid-scream.

Aya whispered protective words Mrs. Holloway had taught her. Chrissy echoed them, her voice shaking.

When the trees finally parted, it was as if they had stumbled into another world.

Before them lay a barren valley, the ground cracked and dry, despite the mist that hung low over it. At its center rose a ruined structure—half-sunken into the earth, covered in black ivy.

The Sanctum.

Aya felt her knees weaken. A force older than the town itself thrummed beneath her feet.

They weren't just standing at the heart of Millers Hollow's secret.

They were standing on a grave.

A deep, shuddering growl vibrated through the ground.

Chrissy turned to her, terror wide in her eyes. "We're not alone."

Something was waking.

And it was hungry.

[End of Chapter 10.]

CHAPTER ELEVEN

The Sanctum Awaits

Aya's heart thundered in her chest, the sound of her own pulse drowning out everything else. They had reached the Sanctum, a place that had been hidden from the world for centuries, but now it was awake—and it was waiting for them.

As they approached the crumbling structure, the air thickened with an eerie, almost tangible energy. Aya could feel it swirling around her, like tendrils of dark smoke wrapping around her body, trying to pull her in.

Suddenly, a sharp pain shot through her head, and her knees buckled. She stumbled but caught herself against the cold stone of the Sanctum's outer wall.

"Aya!" Chrissy shouted, reaching for her. "What's wrong?"

Aya gasped, her breath coming in sharp, ragged bursts. Her vision blurred, and in the midst of the dizziness, she saw a figure. An old woman, dark skin, with silver hair pulled back into an elaborate braid. She was standing

at the edge of a forest, the trees around her
alive with ancient power. But it wasn't just a
vision. The woman was calling to her, her
voice a low murmur that Aya could almost
hear.

"Come, child of the bloodline. The time
has come."

The woman's image flickered, her lips
parting to speak again, but Aya was jolted out
of the vision as Chrissy shook her.

"Aya! What is happening to you?"

Aya blinked, pushing the images away.
Her head was spinning, and the compulsion
to follow the woman's voice was nearly
overwhelming.

"I saw someone," Aya breathed. "An
ancestor, I think. She—" She swallowed hard,
trying to steady herself. "She was calling me.
Telling me the time has come."

Chrissy frowned. "For what?"

Before Aya could respond, the ground
beneath their feet began to tremble. The air
thickened, becoming heavier, suffocating. The
Sanctum was alive—its power growing,

feeding off the blood that coursed through Aya's veins.

"Stay close!" Mrs. Holloway barked, her face pale. She had been quietly observing, but now the gravity of the situation was clear. "Whatever you saw, it's connected to your bloodline, Aya. Your ancestors' past is tied to this place."

Aya felt the weight of Mrs. Holloway's words settle on her shoulders, like a physical force. She had always known she wasn't just another girl in Millers Hollow, but hearing it so plainly made her stomach churn. Her bloodline. The idea made the walls of the world around her feel thinner, as if the earth itself were pressing against her with a pressure that seemed unbearable.

Her blood had been tied to something dark for generations.

They entered the Sanctum.

The first thing that hit Aya was the cold—sharp, bitter cold, like stepping into a tomb that had been sealed shut for millennia. The walls were cracked and covered in thick layers of ivy, but the symbols were still faintly visible. Ancient runes, drawn in a language

Aya couldn't understand, seemed to pulse with a life of their own.

"Stay alert," Mrs. Holloway said, her voice low and strained. "We're on sacred ground now. There's no telling what we'll face inside."

They moved deeper into the Sanctum, the shadows clinging to them like a second skin. Every step Aya took felt heavier than the last. The presence in the air seemed to watch them, its eyes burning into the back of her skull.

And then it happened.

The door at the far end of the Sanctum creaked open, as if it had been waiting for them. Aya felt the pull in her blood, urging her toward it. The closer they got, the more intense the sensation became—like a heartbeat, thumping in her veins, urging her to enter.

She stepped forward, and a wave of dizziness hit her again.

This time, there was no woman.

But there was a memory.

Flashback:

The vision was sharp—clearer than ever before. Aya stood in a clearing, her feet sinking into the soft earth. The air was thick with the scent of herbs and incense. She was no longer in her body; she was the woman from the vision, standing tall in a forest that seemed untouched by time.

"Our ancestors once made a pact to survive," the woman whispered, her voice a soft murmur in the wind. "And now it is our blood that will bind us to this place."

Aya tried to reach out, to speak to her, but the woman only smiled and turned away.

"The curse is not just a past, child. It is a future too. It waits, patient."

With that, the image flickered, and Aya was back in the Sanctum, trembling from the force of the vision.

"Aya!" Chrissy's voice snapped her back to reality, and Aya gasped for air, her heart pounding in her chest.

"What... what did you see?" Chrissy asked, her face pale.

"I saw..." Aya swallowed hard. "I saw her again. The woman from before. She said… the curse isn't just a past. It's a future. It's waiting."

Mrs. Holloway's face darkened. "We don't have much time. The Sanctum is waking, and it's not just your bloodline at risk. It's all of us."

Aya turned toward the door, the pulse in her veins stronger than ever before. There was no turning back now.

They stepped into the inner chamber.

A deep hum resonated from the walls as the door shut behind them, sealing them inside. And at the center of the room was a large stone altar, covered in ancient symbols.

The power in the room was overwhelming, nearly suffocating.

In the center of the altar was a stone book, glowing faintly.

Aya reached for it, her hand trembling.

And as soon as her fingers touched the cover, the room seemed to explode with energy.

[End of Chapter 11.]

CHAPTER TWELVE

The Heart of the Sanctum

Aya's breath hitched in her throat as the stone book pulsed beneath her fingertips. The moment she touched it, an electric current shot through her body, setting every nerve on fire. She jerked her hand back, but the energy did not dissipate. It hummed around her, filling the room with a deafening silence.

The book glowed brighter, its faint light illuminating the room in an otherworldly hue. Aya tried to step back, but something kept her rooted in place, as if the very air was pulling her toward it.

"Aya," Chrissy's voice came through the haze, trembling with urgency. "What's happening? You need to—"

But Aya couldn't hear her. All that mattered was the glowing book, the power within it. It called to her in a voice that was no longer spoken aloud but felt deep in her bones. It knew her. The book knew her.

Suddenly, it was as if time slowed, the air thickening, becoming heavy as though the entire Sanctum had drawn a breath, as if it were alive.

"You are bound to us, child of the bloodline."

The voice came from nowhere, everywhere, and everywhere in between. It was not a voice that could be heard with ears but felt with the soul. Aya's knees buckled, but she steadied herself against the altar, eyes locked on the book.

"I— I don't understand," Aya whispered, her voice shaky.

"The pact that saved your people," the voice continued. "It lives in you. You are its keeper now."

The room around her seemed to swirl, the shadows shifting, coiling like tendrils reaching out to touch her. Aya could see flashes of history—her ancestors, people she didn't know, but felt connected to.

Images of rituals, of sacrifice, of ancient power. She saw herself standing in the same spot, centuries ago, the woman from her visions now clearer than ever. The ancestor who had called to her. This was her—this was her bloodline's legacy.

"Are you ready, Aya?" The voice boomed. "To accept your legacy? To accept the cost?"

Aya gasped, her heart pounding in her chest. The cost. She had never truly considered it. She had always been so focused on surviving, on trying to make sense of the chaos, but now it was clear: she was standing at the precipice of something far greater than she could have imagined.

"Tell me what I have to do," Aya said, her voice stronger now, the weight of her lineage settling over her like an iron cloak.

The air shifted again, growing colder. The ground beneath them rumbled as though the earth was waking from a long slumber. In the center of the room, the stone book began to open, its pages flipping rapidly as if turning themselves.

Aya's eyes were drawn to the pages, to the symbols scrawled in a language she could barely comprehend. But there, amidst the ancient text, she saw something that made her blood run cold.

Her name.

"Aya," the voice said again, softer now, like a lover's whisper. "The time has come for the bloodline to be reborn. You must make the choice: unite the Sanctum's power with your own, or let it slip away forever. There is no middle ground. One will live. One will die."

Her heart stopped. The weight of the decision pressed down on her with the force of an avalanche. She felt as though she were being torn in two, caught between the past and the present, between the living and the dead.

"Is there a way to save everyone?" Aya asked, her voice trembling.

The voice paused, as if considering the question. Then it responded, "Only by fully embracing your bloodline's power."

Aya's chest tightened, but she didn't pull away. She had to know the truth, even if it meant facing the darkest parts of herself. She had to understand her place in all of this.

Her fingers reached out again, but this time, she felt no fear. As her fingers brushed the book's pages, the room erupted in light.

Flashback:

Aya found herself standing in the midst of a forest, not the one she knew, but a place that felt both ancient and alive, full of whispers and shadows. A moon hung high in the sky, its light cold and distant, casting long shadows across the land.

She was no longer herself; she was the ancestor—the same woman she had seen in her visions.

"We are bound by this power," the woman's voice echoed in Aya's mind. "Your bloodline, through time, has carried this curse, this gift. Our ancestors made a pact with the earth itself. They traded their freedom for protection, for power. And now, it is your turn to decide."

Aya's hands trembled as she looked at the altar in front of her. It was the same as the one in the Sanctum. But it was not just stone. It was a portal. A portal that could connect her to the heart of the Sanctum's power.

"Will you follow our path?" the woman whispered. "Will you bind yourself to the Sanctum and its power, to save your people and to destroy our enemies? Or will you abandon us, and let this power fade into nothingness?"

Aya closed her eyes, the weight of the decision suffocating her.

Aya was snapped back to the present, her hand still on the stone book. The words still echoed in her mind.

She felt a presence behind her, and turned to find Mrs. Holloway, her expression grave.

"Aya," she said quietly, her voice full of warning. "You have to be careful. The Sanctum doesn't just give its power freely. If you bind yourself to it, you could lose yourself. The bloodline runs deep, but it's not easy to control."

Aya nodded, but deep down, she already knew. There was no turning back now. She had to take the power. She had to take control.

[End of Chapter 12.]

CHAPTER THIRTEEN

The Price of Power

The book's glow dimmed as Aya's fingers slipped away from its pages. The room felt eerily silent now, the energy receding into the stone walls as though it had never existed. But Aya knew better. The power was still there, lurking beneath the surface, waiting for her to make her final decision.

She turned to face Mrs. Holloway, the gravity of the situation settling heavily on her shoulders. The woman's face was tight with concern, her brow furrowed in a mix of disbelief and fear.

"You don't understand," Mrs. Holloway said softly, almost pleading. "You can't just take the power like that. There are consequences. You don't know what's at stake here, Aya. The Sanctum doesn't give its power freely. It demands everything in return."

Aya swallowed hard, her throat dry as dust. She wanted to argue, to insist that she had no choice, but the words caught in her throat. What if she was wrong? What if she was walking into something far darker than she ever imagined?

"You're right," Aya whispered, almost to herself. "But if I don't take it, then what? What happens to my family? My friends?"

Mrs. Holloway's eyes darkened. "The power doesn't come with just a price; it comes with a curse," she warned. "Your bloodline made a pact, Aya. They traded their souls for protection, for strength, and for secrets hidden within the Sanctum. The cost was always more than they bargained for. And now you have to decide if you're willing to pay that same price."

Aya clenched her fists, the weight of Mrs. Holloway's words sinking in. She had already lost so much. Her life was not her own anymore. But the thought of her people being wiped out, of her legacy disappearing into the void, was something she couldn't bear. The choice felt impossible.

"I don't have a choice," Aya said, her voice low, but resolute. "I have to do this. I have to save them."

Mrs. Holloway's gaze softened, but the warning remained in her eyes. "Then you need to understand something, Aya. When you bind yourself to the Sanctum, you are not just claiming its power. You are becoming its vessel. It will control you as much as you control it. You will lose pieces of yourself— pieces of your humanity—every time you use it."

Aya didn't flinch. She had already lost so much of herself. The power was the only thing that could save her now.

"Tell me what I need to do," Aya said, standing tall. "I'm ready."

Mrs. Holloway sighed, resigned. "Then let's begin."

The Sanctum was a maze of twisting stone halls, its walls heavy with the weight of ancient magic. As they made their way deeper into its bowels, Aya felt the air grow colder, the shadows heavier. The deeper they went, the more it felt like the Sanctum itself was watching her, judging her.

Mrs. Holloway led her to a small chamber, one that Aya had not seen before. The room was circular, its floor etched with strange symbols and runes, glowing faintly in the dim light. In the center of the room was a stone pedestal, and on it rested a blackened dagger, its blade curved like a crescent moon.

"This is the ritual dagger," Mrs. Holloway explained, her voice low and reverent. "It's the key to binding your bloodline to the Sanctum's power. But be warned—it's not a simple sacrifice. This ritual will change you. And once it's done, there's no turning back."

Aya stepped forward, her heart pounding in her chest. She reached for the dagger, her hand trembling as she gripped its cold hilt. The moment her fingers touched the blade, a sharp pain shot through her, and she hissed in surprise.

The dagger began to glow, its runes pulsing with an eerie light. Aya's blood began to hum in her veins, the power of the Sanctum reacting to the touch of its chosen vessel.

"Aya," Mrs. Holloway said softly, her tone urgent. "You need to focus. You have to allow the power to flow through you, to accept it. If you resist, it will destroy you."

Aya nodded, her breathing shallow as the pain intensified. She closed her eyes and let herself sink into the power, letting it wash over her like a tidal wave. The dagger in her hand thrummed with energy, and for a brief moment, she saw flashes of memories—

memories of her ancestors, of their pain and triumph, of their binding to the Sanctum. She felt their voices echo in her mind, their whispered pleas for her to be strong.

"You must be strong, Aya," they said in unison. "The Sanctum will test you. It will try to break you. But you are our bloodline, and you will not falter."

Aya inhaled sharply, her grip on the dagger tightening. She felt her soul stretch, reach out toward the power, and for the first time in her life, she felt like she truly understood her purpose. She was the keeper now. The protector. And the price of that was hers to pay.

With one final breath, Aya drove the dagger into her palm.

The pain was immediate and all-encompassing, a searing fire that consumed her hand and spread up her arm. She felt her body shift, the power coursing through her veins like liquid fire. Her blood burned, but she didn't pull away. She couldn't.

The room around her blurred, as if reality itself were warping. She saw flashes of her family, of people she'd never met, all connected by the same ancient thread. She was part of something bigger, something vast and eternal. The Sanctum's power was inside her now, and she was bound to it forever.

Her vision swam, her body shaking as the energy took hold. For a moment, she thought she might lose herself entirely. The power was overwhelming, and the fear was unbearable. But then, she felt it—an overwhelming sense of control.

Aya opened her eyes, and for the first time, she saw the Sanctum as it truly was— alive, breathing, pulsing with ancient energy. She saw the darkness and the light, the balance between the two forces.

And then, she saw them.

Figures emerged from the shadows— cloaked in black, their eyes burning with malice. Aya's heart raced as she recognized them. The Dark Ones. The ancient enemies of her bloodline. They had been waiting for this moment. Waiting for her to rise.

[End of Chapter 13.]

CHAPTER FOURTEEN

The Shadows Reach

The moment the Dark Ones stepped from the shadows, Aya felt the air shift—becoming thick, oppressive, as if the very atmosphere itself was alive and hungry. She instinctively stepped back, her pulse racing in her chest, but something inside her urged her to stand firm.

She wasn't a victim anymore.

Her fingers twitched at her side, the dagger's energy still buzzing through her palm, and in that instant, she realized the full weight of her decision. The power of the Sanctum was hers, but it wasn't hers alone. It was a force that would change her every moment. Her bloodline had made the bargain centuries ago, but she had paid the price—she had crossed the threshold.

The Dark Ones smiled, their lips curling with malicious pleasure. They were like shadows—figures made of black mist and cruel intentions, their eyes glowing with an unnatural light.

"Well, well," one of them said, his voice a low, gravelly growl that seemed to echo in her mind. "The heir has arrived. We've been waiting for you."

Aya narrowed her eyes, her breath steadying as she clenched the dagger tighter. She wasn't afraid. She couldn't afford to be. She was ready.

"Who are you?" Aya demanded, her voice cold despite the pounding of her heart.

The figure stepped forward, the air around him shimmering with a faint darkness, as though his presence warped reality itself. His eyes burned into hers, and for a moment, she felt her knees weaken. But she forced herself to stand tall.

"We are the Keepers of the Forbidden," the figure replied, his voice carrying a chilling finality. "We are the ones who were cast aside by your ancestors. The ones who were bound in the deepest parts of the Sanctum. And we are here to take back what was stolen from us."

Aya's gaze flickered to Mrs. Holloway, who stood behind her, her expression grim. "They're the ones... they were sealed away," Mrs. Holloway murmured, barely audible.

"Your bloodline was tasked with keeping them in check, Aya. But now... now they've come to reclaim their power."

Aya's mind raced, the pieces of the puzzle starting to fall into place. The Sanctum was more than just a repository of power—it was a prison, a containment for forces darker than she could have imagined. And her bloodline had been the warden.

But no more.

Aya stepped forward, the dagger held firmly in her grasp. "I won't let you."

The Dark One in front of her chuckled, a sound that echoed in the chamber like nails dragging across stone. "You think you can stop us?" he mocked, his figure shifting like smoke. "You don't even understand the power you've claimed, little girl. The Sanctum is not just an ally; it is a master. You will bend to it. All of you will."

Aya felt the pull of the power within her, the deep, primal force that surged through her veins. It whispered to her, calling to her— urging her to surrender, to give in to the dark side that was slowly taking root inside her.

She could feel it—feel it clawing at her, trying to take over. The dagger pulsed in her hand, its energy overwhelming her senses. The shadows around her grew deeper, and the Dark Ones began to encircle her, their forms flickering in and out of the light.

But Aya resisted. She wouldn't succumb.

With a swift motion, she plunged the dagger into the ground, letting the energy explode outward. The force of it shook the room, sending ripples through the air. The Dark Ones staggered back, their bodies flickering as the blast of power rippled through them.

The shadows screamed, their forms twisting in agony.

But Aya didn't stop. She couldn't. The Sanctum's power surged through her, as though her body had become a conduit for its raw, untamed energy. The runes etched into the stone walls began to glow brighter, their ancient magic responding to her call.

She could hear the voices of her ancestors again—rising with her, urging her forward.

"You are the vessel, Aya. You are the key."

With every word they spoke, the power inside her grew stronger, more focused. She raised her arms, calling the power to her, feeling it pulse in her fingertips.

The Dark Ones screeched, their eyes wide with terror. "No!" they cried in unison. "This is impossible! You can't control it!"

But Aya smiled, her heart alight with a fire she had never known. She could control it.

And then, she did the unthinkable.

Aya thrust her hand forward, unleashing the full force of the Sanctum's power.

The air cracked with the sound of an ancient bond breaking, the walls of the Sanctum trembling under the intensity of the magical forces colliding. Aya's mind reeled as the power tore through the chamber, the shadows dissolving into the air as the Dark Ones howled in agony. They tried to resist, but the power of the Sanctum was unstoppable once she had claimed it.

The room fell silent.

Aya stood in the center of the chamber, panting heavily, her heart racing as the power slowly faded from her. She looked around, her gaze searching for any sign of the Dark Ones. But they were gone. Vanished. Their presence erased.

Mrs. Holloway slowly approached, her expression one of awe and fear. "You did it," she whispered, her voice shaking. "You truly did it."

Aya's eyes were wide, but she felt no triumph. She had won, yes. But at what cost? She could feel the power still stirring inside her, still alive and hungry. And deep inside, she knew this was only the beginning.

The Sanctum had chosen her, but it hadn't just chosen her to wield its power. It had chosen her as its guardian.

And now, she was bound to it—whether she liked it or not.

[End of Chapter 14.]

CHAPTER FIFTEEN

The Two Paths

Aya could feel the weight of the book in her hands as she climbed back up the stairs, the whispers of the past curling around her like smoke. The decision she was about to face was bigger than her, bigger than the house, bigger than any battle she'd fought so far.

As she emerged from the dark stairwell, Chrissy stood at the top, her eyes wide with concern.

"Aya, what did you see down there?" she asked, voice trembling. "What's going on?"

Aya swallowed hard, trying to push away the fear clawing at her chest. She didn't have all the answers — but one thing was clear: this wasn't just about surviving. It was about choosing who she was going to become.

"Everything," Aya whispered. "And nothing good."

She held the book up, the symbols on the cover glowing faintly in the dim light of the room. "It's a record of my family's pact. Our bloodline. The dark power we were bound to generations ago. It's— it's more than just stories. It's... a debt that still needs to be paid."

Chrissy's face paled. "A debt? Aya, what do you mean?"

Aya closed her eyes, her thoughts spiraling. She didn't know how to explain the pull she felt toward the power inside her. It was seductive, demanding. But the price... the price was always blood.

"The bloodline," Aya murmured, "was never meant to be a gift. It was a curse. One that started long before me... and one that will follow me until I choose."

Chrissy stepped forward, placing a hand on Aya's arm. "Aya, you don't have to do this. We can walk away. We can run—"

"No," Aya interrupted, shaking her head. "I can't run from this. It's in me. I can feel it." She took a deep breath, the air thick with the weight of the decision. "But there's a choice to make. The book... it shows two paths. One of light. One of darkness."

The room felt colder, as though the walls themselves were holding their breath. Aya opened the book to the page that had haunted her earlier, the page that depicted the crossroads — the girl standing at the fork, her future torn between two paths.

The first path shimmered with the promise of light — of control, of peace, of strength earned through sacrifice. The second path, darker, called with a different kind of power — one of domination, fear, and control.

"This is bigger than me, Chrissy," Aya said, voice strained. "It's about more than just surviving. It's about deciding who I'll become. The curse is already inside me, and the path I choose will decide the future of this bloodline."

Chrissy swallowed hard. "But Aya, how can you even choose between those two? The darkness... it's dangerous. It'll consume you. You saw what it did to the others."

Aya bit her lip. "I saw what it could do. But what if... what if the darkness can be controlled? What if I can use it to protect everyone else?"

The question hung in the air, heavy with the weight of its implications. The truth was, Aya wasn't sure anymore what the right path was. She couldn't ignore the hunger in her veins, the magic that surged inside her whenever she called upon it. But the cost? The cost was more than she could bear.

"Aya, whatever path you choose, I'm with you," Chrissy said, her voice unwavering. "But don't let the darkness swallow you whole."

Aya nodded, the resolve in her heart hardening. "I won't. I'll find a way to walk the line. I'll find a way to control it."

But deep down, she knew the hardest part was yet to come. The path of light was tempting, but it felt too... uncertain. Too fragile. The darkness, on the other hand, was powerful. It was easy to see how someone could fall under its sway.

A scream echoed through the house, pulling Aya and Chrissy from their thoughts. It was distant — a cry of pain and desperation. But it was enough to pull them back into the fight.

"Aya..." Chrissy started, her voice low. "The hunters. They're coming."

Aya's heart raced. She didn't have time for second-guessing.

She closed the book with a snap, shoving it into her jacket. "We have to move. Now."

The two girls rushed out of the house, the storm still raging around them. The wind howled like a wild animal, and the streets were flooded with rain. But the real danger wasn't the storm.

The real danger was the hunters.

"They're too close," Aya muttered, scanning the dark streets. "They know where we are. They'll be here any minute."

"I don't care," Chrissy snapped. "We fight back. We're not running anymore."

Aya didn't argue. They had no time to waste. They had to take the fight to the hunters — and, maybe, in doing so, find the answers they both desperately needed.

But as they moved, something in the back of Aya's mind whispered again.

The paths were coming closer. The time to choose was almost here.

[End of Chapter 15.]

CHAPTER SIXTEEN

Into the Abyss

The Sanctum pulsed with a force that Aya could feel deep in her bones. It had been days since she first embraced the full power of the ancient magic, and the change within her was undeniable. Every step she took was infused with energy, every breath felt like an extension of the force that had become a part of her. She could feel the weight of the power coursing through her veins, sometimes overwhelming, sometimes invigorating.

But with the power came a deeper understanding of its dangers. The Order of the Forsaken was real, and they were coming for her. Their presence loomed in the distance like a dark cloud gathering strength. Aya had heard whispers, seen their symbols etched in the dark corners of her dreams, and felt their influence stirring in the very air around her.

Her mind kept returning to the cryptic warning Mrs. Holloway had given her—Only when you embrace the Sanctum will you be able to face them. It had seemed so simple, so clear at the time. Now, the weight of those words crushed her. The deeper she sank into the magic, the more she felt herself losing touch with the world she once knew. It was as if the power was calling her, urging her to transcend the limits of humanity, to step into something... other.

"Aya," Mrs. Holloway's voice broke through her thoughts, and Aya's head snapped around.

The older woman stood in the doorway of the Sanctum's chamber, her eyes shadowed with concern. "We don't have much time. They're closer than you think."

Aya's heart tightened. She could feel the pull of the magic growing stronger, but there was something in Mrs. Holloway's voice—a sense of urgency—that snapped her back to reality.

"Then we have to act," Aya said, her voice steady, though the dread pooling in her stomach threatened to undo her. She wasn't sure how long she could resist the power, how long she could keep herself from fully surrendering to it. She didn't want to lose herself in the Sanctum's depths. But she also knew that she couldn't afford to hesitate.

Mrs. Holloway stepped closer, her expression a mix of determination and sorrow. "I've been in contact with some of the other guardians," she said, her words low and urgent. "They've heard the stirrings of the Order. They're coming for the Sanctum. They want the power, and they believe you're the key to unlocking it."

Aya nodded grimly. She had suspected as much. The Order of the Forsaken didn't just want the Sanctum's power—they wanted control of it. They wanted to manipulate it, twist it to their own ends.

"You said the only way to stop them was to embrace the power completely," Aya said. "How do I do that?"

Mrs. Holloway's face softened, and for a moment, Aya saw the weight of centuries in her eyes. "You must descend into the heart of the Sanctum," she said. "There, you will face your own darkness. You must confront the parts of yourself you fear, the parts that the power will bring to the surface. If you can overcome that, then you will fully understand the Sanctum—and yourself."

Aya shuddered. The idea of facing her own darkness was terrifying, but she knew it was necessary. She had no choice but to move forward.

"I'm ready," Aya said, her voice unwavering.

Mrs. Holloway's lips pressed together, as if holding back a thousand unsaid words. Finally, she nodded. "Then go. The longer you wait, the stronger the Order grows. You have to face this, Aya, before they do."

Aya didn't waste another moment. She turned toward the inner chamber of the Sanctum, the ancient door groaning as it slowly opened. A gust of cool air washed over her, and she stepped forward into the shadows, where the pulse of power was strongest.

The further she went, the darker it became. The walls of the Sanctum closed in around her, the air growing thick with magic. Aya could feel the weight of every step, each one pulling her deeper into the unknown. Her breath came in shallow gasps as she navigated the winding corridors, each turn leading her further into the heart of the Sanctum.

At the end of the hall, a massive door loomed in front of her. It was made of dark stone, etched with ancient runes that glowed faintly in the dim light. Aya knew this was the place. This was where she would face the darkness within herself.

She reached out and pressed her hand against the cold surface of the door. Immediately, the runes flared to life, a surge of energy shooting through her arm. The door groaned, opening slowly as the magic wrapped around her like a familiar embrace.

Aya stepped inside. The chamber was unlike anything she had ever seen. It was vast, the walls stretching far beyond what her eyes could see, filled with swirling shadows and flickering lights. The air was thick with energy, so thick that it felt as though it were pressing against her skin.

In the center of the room stood a pedestal, a single black stone resting upon it. It was small, no bigger than her hand, but Aya could feel its power from where she stood. This was the heart of the Sanctum. This was the source of all the magic she had tapped into.

But as she moved toward it, the shadows around the room shifted. Figures began to materialize in the dark, their forms twisting and shifting like smoke. Aya's heart raced. She wasn't alone.

Out of the shadows stepped a figure she recognized. It was herself—her reflection, but distorted, twisted in ways that made her stomach churn. The other version of her smiled cruelly.

"You think you can control this power?" the twisted version of Aya asked, her voice mocking. "You can't. It will consume you, just as it consumed all the others before you."

Aya's heart hammered in her chest as she took a step back, unsure of what to do. The figure in front of her was a part of her, wasn't it? A manifestation of her fear, her doubts, her darkness.

"You're not real," Aya said, trying to steady her shaking hands. "You're just a part of me."

The twisted version of herself laughed, the sound cold and haunting. "Is that what you tell yourself? That you can control this? That you're stronger than it? You're already losing, Aya. You just don't see it yet."

Aya's breath hitched as she took another step back. The figure's words stung with an uncomfortable truth. How much of herself was she willing to give up in order to wield this power? Could she truly control it without losing who she was?

The answer came in the form of a sharp, burning pain in her chest. Aya gasped, clutching her heart as the power inside her surged out of control. It was too much. She couldn't contain it. It was slipping through her fingers, consuming her from the inside out.

But then she remembered Mrs. Holloway's words. She had to face her darkness. She had to confront her fears.

Aya closed her eyes, reaching deep inside herself. She allowed the darkness to rise, allowed the power to flow freely through her. She would not fight it. She would embrace it. It was a part of her now.

With a final, steadying breath, Aya opened her eyes. The twisted version of herself faded away, melting into the shadows as the power within her settled. The pain subsided, leaving only a deep, abiding strength. Aya stood tall, her body glowing with the magic of the Sanctum. She had embraced it. She had become one with it. But the danger wasn't over yet.

[End of Chapter 16.]

CHAPTER SEVENTEEN

The Coming Storm

The air outside the Sanctum crackled with tension as Aya emerged from the chamber, her body pulsing with raw power. She had faced her darkness, embraced the magic that had threatened to consume her, and emerged stronger for it. But that strength came with a price—a weight that she now carried with her. Her mind, once clear and focused, felt clouded, torn between the light of her humanity and the pull of the magic that now lived within her.

She stepped into the central hall of the Sanctum, where Mrs. Holloway was waiting. The older woman's eyes narrowed as she took in Aya's appearance—the way the air seemed to hum around her, the faint glow that radiated from her skin.

"You've done it," Mrs. Holloway said, her voice tinged with both pride and concern. "But I fear the worst is yet to come."

Aya nodded, her gaze far away. She had felt the change inside herself, the way the magic flowed more easily now, like a second heartbeat. But with that power came the knowledge of the coming storm. She could feel the Order's presence, creeping closer with every passing moment. They were coming for her, coming for the Sanctum, and Aya knew that there was no more running.

"I'm ready," Aya said, her voice steady but laced with a quiet determination.

Mrs. Holloway's face softened, but there was no mistaking the sadness in her eyes. "No one is ever truly ready for this," she replied, her tone grave. "The Order of the Forsaken is relentless. They will stop at nothing to claim the Sanctum's power. And once they have it…" Her words trailed off, but the implication was clear. If the Order took control of the Sanctum, they would wield the magic to reshape the world in their twisted image. The consequences would be catastrophic.

"We can't let that happen," Aya said firmly. "I won't let it happen."

Mrs. Holloway gave a solemn nod. "Then we must prepare. The battle is coming, Aya.

You'll need to be more than just the magic. You'll need to use every part of yourself— your mind, your will, your heart. It's not just about power; it's about who you are and what you stand for."

Aya's heart raced at the thought of the battle ahead. The Order was cunning, powerful, and they wouldn't hesitate to destroy anyone in their way. But Aya had something they didn't—a deep connection to the Sanctum, an understanding of the magic they sought to control. She wouldn't let them tear that away from her.

"We don't have much time," Mrs. Holloway continued. "I'll gather the other guardians. We need to make sure the Sanctum is protected. You'll have to face the Order alone when they come for you. But you won't be without aid."

Aya looked at Mrs. Holloway, her eyes burning with resolve. "I'm ready. Let's end this."

Hours later, the Sanctum was alive with preparation. The guardians moved quickly, their faces grim, knowing the battle ahead was one they might not survive. Aya, however, couldn't afford to think about that. She had faced her own darkness, but the thought of losing everyone she had come to care about haunted her. She had to fight—not just for herself, but for the future of the Sanctum and everyone within it.

Mrs. Holloway, now joined by several other guardians, briefed Aya on the tactics they would use to hold off the Order. But as they discussed, Aya's mind kept drifting to the vision she had seen deep within the Sanctum's heart. A vision of her standing against the Order, the power of the Sanctum flowing through her like an unstoppable tide. The image was both inspiring and terrifying.

"You're not alone in this, Aya," one of the guardians, a tall man named Kaden, said as he approached her. His expression was serious but filled with a quiet strength. "The Sanctum's magic has always been a force for good, but it needs someone who understands its balance. If anyone can control it, it's you."

Aya nodded, though doubts lingered in the back of her mind. Could she really control the Sanctum's magic? Could she truly wield it against the Order without losing herself to it? Every instinct told her to trust in her strength, but the power coursing through her veins was volatile. It was easy to get lost in it, to let it take over completely.

As the sun dipped below the horizon, the temperature in the Sanctum's heart dropped, and the air grew thick with the impending sense of battle. The moment of confrontation was near.

"They're here," Mrs. Holloway said, her voice a whisper of dread. The tension in the room ratcheted up as everyone took their positions.

Aya stood at the heart of the Sanctum, her hands outstretched as she focused on the magic within her. She could feel it thrumming beneath her skin, responding to her call. The Sanctum was alive with energy, and she could feel its heartbeat synchronize with her own. This was her time.

"Are you ready?" Mrs. Holloway asked, her voice filled with a mixture of pride and concern.

Aya took a deep breath, her gaze steady. "I was born ready."

Outside, the air had gone still, and the ground trembled beneath the weight of the approaching Order. Aya could feel them now, their presence looming over the Sanctum like a dark cloud. The Order of the Forsaken was no longer a shadow in the distance. They were here, and they were coming for everything Aya had fought to protect.

The door to the Sanctum slammed open with a deafening crash, and the Order poured into the room, their dark robes swirling around them like smoke. Their leader, a tall figure cloaked in shadow, stepped forward, his eyes gleaming with malevolent intent.

"Aya," he said, his voice cold and venomous. "You're the key to unlocking the Sanctum's true power. Surrender, and we'll spare your life."

Aya's heart thundered in her chest, but she stood tall, refusing to give in. "I won't let you take it," she said, her voice unwavering. "This power is mine to protect."

The leader of the Order laughed, a harsh, cruel sound. "You think you can stop us? You have no idea what you're dealing with."

Aya's mind raced as she prepared for the inevitable battle. She could feel the weight of the Sanctum's power pressing against her, but she also knew that it wasn't enough to rely solely on magic. She would need to fight with everything she had.

With a wave of her hand, Aya summoned the Sanctum's magic, the air around her crackling with energy. The Order's leader raised his hand, and the room shook with a surge of dark power. The battle for the Sanctum had begun.

[End of Chapter 17.]

CHAPTER EIGHTEEN

Ashes of the Past

The ruined church stood at the top of the hill, swallowed by tangled vines and the heavy breath of the night. The mist that hung low over the ground seemed to shy away from its broken steeple, as if even the elements remembered what had been done here.

Aya clutched Chrissy's hand as they approached, their steps muffled by the thick layer of leaves and dirt. Each breath they took was damp, the air soaked in a sadness too old to name.

The heavy wooden doors swung open with a protesting groan when Aya pushed them. Inside, shadows writhed along the charred walls, and every broken pew seemed to bow in mourning. The altar at the far end was a heap of ash and splintered wood.

"This place..." Chrissy whispered, her voice trembling. "It's like it's alive."

Aya nodded, swallowing the lump in her throat. She could feel it too — a heartbeat in the walls, a breath in the floorboards. It was waiting for them.

As they stepped inside, a sudden gust slammed the doors shut behind them. Aya jumped, spinning around, but Chrissy squeezed her hand tighter.

"Stay with me," she said. Her wide, dark eyes reflected the glimmers of unseen movement deeper inside the church.

They moved forward, their steps slow, each footfall echoing in the oppressive silence. Chrissy's hand brushed a half-burned hymnal, and it disintegrated into dust under her fingertips.

When they reached the altar, they knelt and dug carefully through the debris. Beneath it, nestled in a hollow of blackened stone, lay a locket.

Aya picked it up. The moment her fingers touched it, a jolt shot through her — a flood of images, sounds, emotions not her own. She gasped.

Inside the locket were two faded photographs — women who looked hauntingly like them.

"Our ancestors," Aya whispered.

Before Chrissy could answer, the ground trembled beneath them. A low hum filled the church, growing louder until it became a chorus of voices—whispering, crying, chanting in a tongue Aya couldn't understand.

Figures began to form from the mist—ghostly shapes clothed in robes, their faces hidden by shadows. Some clutched ancient symbols. Others carried weapons made of bone and iron.

Chrissy stumbled back, but Aya caught her. "No," Aya said. "We can't run. They're not here to kill us. They're here because we woke them."

The spirits circled them, faster now, their whispers growing urgent.

Suddenly, one figure broke from the circle—a woman with wild silver hair and piercing eyes. She pointed directly at Aya.

"Blood of my blood," she intoned. "The curse is not yet broken. The price has not been paid."

The other spirits echoed her words in a bone-chilling chant. Aya's head spun. She gripped the locket so tightly it bit into her palm.

"What price?" Chrissy shouted above the din. "What are you talking about?"

The silver-haired spirit reached into the folds of her robes and drew out a dagger — old, chipped, but thrumming with power. She held it out to Aya.

"Choose," she commanded. "Seal your fate... or free the bloodline."

Aya stared at the dagger, then at Chrissy. Her heart thundered in her chest.

"What do we do?" Chrissy whispered.

Before Aya could answer, another figure—a man whose face was scarred and burning with hatred—lunged from the shadows, shrieking.

"Run!" Aya shouted, shoving Chrissy back.

The spirit's hand grazed Aya's shoulder, and pain seared through her, white-hot and unbearable. Aya screamed, stumbling to her knees. Visions flooded her mind—burning crosses, screaming women, chains binding wrists and ankles. The horrors her ancestors endured poured into her.

Chrissy grabbed a broken piece of wood and swung it wildly at the spirit, passing through it harmlessly. But it distracted him enough for Aya to stagger upright.

"We need to get out!" Chrissy yelled.

"No," Aya gasped. "We have to finish it."

Summoning every ounce of strength, Aya grabbed the dagger from the spirit woman's outstretched hand. The metal pulsed against her skin, filling her veins with fire.

The chanting stopped.

Silence fell, so heavy it felt like the world had been muffled. The spirits stood still, watching.

Aya raised the dagger high and plunged it into the altar.

A deafening crack split the air. The ground shook violently, and a bolt of blinding white light shot up through the ruins, shattering what was left of the roof.

The spirits screamed—not in anger, but in release. One by one, they dissolved into streams of silver light that twisted upward into the night sky.

Aya collapsed against Chrissy, panting, the locket still burning hot against her skin.

It was over.

Or so they thought.

As they staggered out of the church into the open air, Aya glanced back once.

Deep in the ruins, where the altar once stood, a single ember still glowed, pulsing like a heartbeat.

And somewhere, far away, something woke up.

[End of Chapter 18.]

CHAPTER NINETEEN

Whispers Beneath the Skin

The night air was thick and buzzing when Aya and Chrissy stumbled down the hill away from the ruined church. Sweat and ash clung to their skin, and the adrenaline still racing through their veins made their limbs shake uncontrollably.

They didn't speak — couldn't. There were no words yet big enough to contain what they had just seen.

Behind them, the old church sagged deeper into itself, the faint glow of the ember still visible like a cursed star on the blackened landscape.

When they reached the base of the hill, Chrissy finally spoke.

"Aya... did we really end it?" Her voice cracked, the edges fraying with fear and exhaustion.

Aya clutched the locket tighter, feeling its weight against her chest. It no longer burned, but it pulsed, like it had fused with her heartbeat.

"I don't know," Aya said honestly. "It felt like something broke... but something else woke up."

Chrissy looked back over her shoulder, shivering. "I felt it too."

The streets were strangely empty as they made their way back toward Aya's house. A heavy stillness hung in the air — not peace, but waiting.

Every shadow seemed to move. Every whisper of wind seemed to carry voices just beyond understanding.

They hadn't just stirred up the past. They had ripped open something that had been buried for generations.

By the time they reached Aya's street, their exhaustion weighed on them like a physical force. But as they approached the house, Aya skidded to a halt.

The front door was ajar.

A slow creak as it moved slightly in the breeze.

Chrissy caught her arm. "Aya..."

Without thinking, Aya grabbed the heavy flashlight from Chrissy's backpack and crept up the steps. The door moaned on its hinges as she pushed it open wider.

The house was dark. Silent. Too silent.

Aya's heart pounded against her ribs as she stepped inside. The air was cold, unnaturally so, and the familiar smells of home — cinnamon, old wood, laundry detergent — were drowned under a sour, metallic tang.

They edged into the living room, Aya sweeping the flashlight around.

That's when they saw it.

The walls — once warm with family portraits — were now covered in frantic scratches. Deep gouges, as if someone had taken a knife or claws to the paint, carving symbols that twisted and writhed in the light.

Blood. The symbols were drawn in blood.

Chrissy gagged behind her hand.

Aya's knees buckled, but she forced herself forward. She recognized some of the symbols. She had seen them in old books, whispered about in the forbidden margins of history. Symbols for binding. For summoning.

For control.

On the floor, in the center of the living room, a small mound of ashes and burnt paper sat within a circle of salt.

Aya bent down, her breath catching in her throat. She picked up a charred scrap of parchment from the ashes.

On it, barely visible, were words written in an ancient dialect.
But even without translating, Aya understood the message.

"We are not finished."

A cold hand closed around her wrist.

Aya screamed, jerking back — but there was no one there.

Chrissy grabbed her. "We have to get out! Now!"

Aya nodded, heart hammering. They raced out the door, stumbling onto the porch just as the air inside seemed to shudder and collapse inward — like the house was breathing, sucking them back in.

The door slammed shut behind them.

They didn't look back.

They ran.

They didn't stop running until they reached Chrissy's car, parked half a block away. Breathless and shaking, Chrissy fumbled with the keys.

"Aya," she gasped. "What the hell was that?! What does it mean?"

Aya didn't answer right away. Her mind was racing, piecing together fragments of what she had seen in the visions, what the spirits had tried to tell her.

"It means..." Aya finally said, staring into the darkness around them, "that the bloodline isn't just bound by memory or pain."

"It's bound by something alive."

Chrissy stared at her. "Alive?"

Aya nodded grimly. "Something they tried to destroy long ago. But it never died.

It's in us. It's in our blood. And now... it's awake."

The car's headlights flickered on.
In the rearview mirror, for just a split second, Aya saw a figure standing in the middle of the street behind them — too tall, too thin, its face a blurred smear of shadow.

Then it was gone.

But Aya knew better.

This was only the beginning.

[End of Chapter 19.]

CHAPTER TWENTY

Echoes of the Forgotten

The rain started as a whisper.

Fat, heavy drops splattered against the windshield as Chrissy sped through the empty streets, the wipers working furiously to clear their view. The storm had been building for hours, a slow pressure that now burst in a cold deluge.

Aya sat in the passenger seat, her fingers clenched so tightly around the locket that her knuckles turned white.
It thrummed against her palm, alive with a strange warmth.

"We can't go back to your house," Chrissy said, glancing at her. "Not after... that."

Aya shook her head. "No. We need to find answers first. Before whatever that was finds us."

Chrissy bit her lip, considering. "We could go to my grandmother's. She... she used to talk about things like this. Old protections. Old magic."

Aya turned to her sharply. "Why didn't you say anything before?"

Chrissy's cheeks flushed. "Because I thought she was just a crazy old woman. Talking about spirits in the water and names you weren't supposed to say out loud."

Aya's mind raced. "No. She's exactly what we need."

The rain pounded harder as they swerved onto the old highway that led out toward the countryside. Trees lined the road, their skeletal limbs clawing at the sky.

It felt like the world was holding its breath.

Twenty minutes later, they pulled up in front of a battered two-story house. The porch light was out, but faint glimmers shone through the curtains inside.

Chrissy cut the engine, and they sat in silence for a moment, the rain drumming around them like a warning.

"You sure about this?" Aya asked.

Chrissy hesitated, then nodded. "If anyone can help us... it's her."

They sprinted to the porch, Aya clutching the locket to her chest. Chrissy banged on the door.

A long pause.

Then the door creaked open, revealing a small woman wrapped in layers of shawls and scarves. Her hair was silver, her eyes sharp and unnervingly clear.

She peered at them for a moment — and then, without a word, ushered them inside.

The house smelled of herbs, smoke, and old wood. Strange symbols adorned the walls. Small bundles of dried flowers hung from the ceiling.

The old woman — Chrissy called her Mémé — led them to the sitting room, where a low fire crackled in the hearth.

"You've stirred them," Mémé said without preamble, her voice a rasp like wind through dead leaves.

Aya swallowed hard. "Stirred what?"

"The Forgotten," Mémé said simply. "The ones who were bound but never freed. Your blood carries their memory. Their anger."

Aya and Chrissy exchanged a look.

Mémé's gaze sharpened. "You think you destroyed them at the church? Foolish girls. You only weakened the chains."

She reached out, her gnarled fingers brushing the locket. The moment she touched it, a low hum filled the air.

"This," she said, her voice low and reverent, "is not just a relic. It is a beacon. A key."

Aya's heart thudded painfully. "A key to what?"

Mémé leaned closer. "To everything they tried to hide. To the true source of their power. And now that it's active, the Forgotten will hunt you. They will not rest until they reclaim what was stolen from them."

Chrissy shivered. "What do we do?"

Mémé studied them for a long moment. "You must go where it all began. The place where the first binding was done. Only there can you sever the blood tie — or forge it into something stronger."

Aya's voice trembled. "Where?"

Mémé smiled grimly. "Beneath the river. In the drowned village."

Aya felt the world tilt beneath her feet.

The drowned village.
She had heard stories growing up — whispers of a settlement that had been wiped from the maps, flooded decades ago under the pretense of creating a reservoir.
But the elders spoke of something darker.
Of people who had vanished. Of rituals interrupted.

Now she knew the truth: the village hadn't just been flooded to build a reservoir. It had been buried. To hide what they couldn't destroy.

Mémé pressed a small, leather-bound book into Aya's hands. The cover was cracked and worn.

"You'll need this," she said. "The river guards its secrets well. Only the marked blood can find the way."

Aya opened the book. Inside were maps, spells, and warnings written in languages she barely recognized.

She looked up, fear and determination warring inside her.

"We'll find it," she said. "We'll finish what they started."

Mémé's eyes gleamed. "Be careful, child. Some bloodlines do not want to be unbound."

As they left the house, the rain finally stopped.

The clouds parted just enough to reveal a sliver of the moon — pale and watchful.

Aya tightened her grip on the book and the locket.

The drowned village waited.
And with it, the final truth of her bloodline.

Whatever it cost, she would uncover it.

No matter what hunted her through the darkness.

[End of Chapter 20.]

CHAPTER TWENTY-ONE

Into the Depths

The road to the reservoir was long and silent.

Chrissy gripped the steering wheel tightly, knuckles pale. Aya sat beside her, the locket and the leather-bound book resting in her lap. The faint hum of the locket never stopped now — it was a steady vibration in her hands, as if it was eager, urging her forward.

The world around them changed as they drove.
The paved streets gave way to cracked asphalt, then to gravel roads surrounded by thick forests. Civilization fell away behind them, swallowed by mist and shadow.

The drowned village waited beyond the reservoir — somewhere below the water, where no light reached.

"I can't believe this is real," Chrissy whispered, her voice barely audible over the rumble of the engine.

Aya didn't answer. She stared out the window, watching as the trees leaned closer, their branches heavy with rainwater. Everything felt different out here — older, untouched.

As if something ancient still lingered.

They parked near the edge of the reservoir.

The water was black under the cloudy sky, perfectly still, reflecting nothing. A faint mist hovered above the surface, swirling in strange patterns.

"This is it," Chrissy said, shivering despite the thick jacket she wore.

Aya opened the book Mémé had given her. The map inside showed a hidden path, one that supposedly led down beneath the waterline, into the remains of the village.

"There's supposed to be an entrance," Aya said, tracing the faded ink with her finger. "An old chapel that wasn't fully submerged."

"You're telling me we have to go under that?" Chrissy asked, wide-eyed.

Aya nodded grimly. "It's the only way."

They followed the treeline, staying low, their flashlights barely piercing the heavy mist. The locket tugged against Aya's neck, a subtle pull in one direction.

Guiding her.

Finally, they spotted it: a crumbling stone archway half-buried in mud and moss, jutting out from the bank like a broken tooth.
The chapel.

They approached carefully.

The entrance was narrow, almost hidden by overgrowth. Faint carvings covered the stone — symbols Aya recognized from the book: seals of protection, meant to keep things in, not out.

"This is insane," Chrissy muttered. "If we die down there, I'm haunting you."

Aya gave a weak smile. "Deal."

They slipped inside.

The air was colder inside the chapel. Thick with dampness and the scent of earth and decay.

Their flashlight beams revealed ruined pews, a collapsed altar, and at the very back — a staircase descending into darkness.

Aya swallowed hard.
This was it.

The descent was slow. The stairs slick with moisture, crumbling under their weight. The walls closed in around them, the only sound their breathing and the soft squelch of water underfoot.

Then — movement.

A shadow at the edge of their light.
Gone before they could focus on it.

Chrissy grabbed Aya's arm. "Tell me that was just my imagination."

Aya didn't answer.
Because she saw it too.

The staircase ended in a flooded corridor.

Water lapped at their ankles, cold as ice. The locket pulsed harder, vibrating against Aya's chest.

"This way," she said, heart pounding.

The corridor twisted and turned. Doors lined the walls, some ripped off their hinges, others sealed shut with rotting wood. Murmured whispers floated through the air — voices that shouldn't exist.

They ignored them.
They had to.

At the very end of the corridor, they found it: a door marked with the same symbol as the locket.

Aya reached for it.

The instant her fingers touched the wood, the whispers turned into screams.

The door burst open.

Beyond the door was a cavernous space — part of the old village, somehow preserved beneath the reservoir. Dilapidated buildings leaned at odd angles, streets flooded ankle-deep.

And in the center of it all stood a massive tree, gnarled and blackened, its roots sinking deep into the earth.

The locket burned against Aya's skin.

"This is it," she whispered.

The heart of the village.
The source of the bloodline's power.

But even as she spoke,
something shifted in the dark water around
them.
Shapes began to rise — figures half-formed,
their faces blurred, their bodies dripping with
black sludge.

The Forgotten.

And they were waiting.

Aya and Chrissy backed up instinctively,
but there was nowhere to run.

The locket glowed fiercely, casting harsh
light across the cavern.

The figures stopped, hissing, retreating
slightly from the glow.

"They're afraid of it," Chrissy said.

Aya nodded. "We have to use it."

She pulled the book from her bag,
flipping through the pages until she found it
— a ritual written in old ink, meant to either
sever the bloodline's cursed tie or claim its full
power.

Her hands trembled.

If they failed, they would be trapped here — just like the others.

"Stay close to me," Aya said.

Together, they stepped toward the black tree, the Forgotten howling around them, the cavern trembling under the weight of old sins finally waking.

The final battle had begun.

[End of Chapter 21.]

CHAPTER TWENTY-TWO

The Choice Beneath

The cavern shook as Aya and Chrissy approached the blackened tree, its roots writhing as if alive.
The screams of the Forgotten echoed off the stone walls, creating a dizzying roar that made it hard to think.

Chrissy clutched Aya's arm tightly. "Whatever you're going to do," she gasped, "do it fast."

Aya knelt at the base of the tree, the leather-bound book open before her.
The locket blazed in her hands, its heat almost unbearable.

The ritual was written in ancient Creole, words Aya could barely understand — but somehow, in the pit of her soul, she knew what they meant.

The blood in her veins remembered.

Two paths. Two fates.

One ritual would destroy the bloodline's curse — sever the tie to this power forever. The other would claim it, binding the full strength of the old magic to Aya alone, but at a terrible cost: her soul would never truly be her own again.

The ground beneath them cracked, black water seeping up through the broken stone.

The Forgotten howled louder, some clawing toward them, some sinking back into the water as if in fear.

Chrissy leaned down beside Aya, her voice trembling. "We can't stay here. Pick one!"

Aya stared at the pages, heart pounding. Her mother's face flashed before her eyes. Her grandmother.
Mémé.
All the generations before her who had carried the burden... who had suffered.

Was she strong enough to destroy it?
Or would she fall into the same trap — lured by the promise of power?

The locket pulsed harder, urging her toward the destructive path.
But deep inside, something else — a softer

pull — whispered of freedom, of ending the cycle forever.

Aya gritted her teeth.

She chose.

Lifting the locket high, she began to chant the words for severance.

The cavern reacted instantly.
The tree screeched — an inhuman, bone-rattling sound — as cracks raced up its trunk, splitting it apart.

The Forgotten shrieked, writhing, their forms flickering like dying flames.

Water poured in from the reservoir above, rushing down the walls in thick sheets.

Chrissy grabbed Aya's hand. "Aya, MOVE!"

The two of them sprinted, slipping on the wet stone, as the cavern collapsed around them.
The tree splintered, exploding into a million shards of dark wood and mist.

The locket shattered in Aya's hand, releasing a blinding flash of light that knocked them both off their feet.

Aya coughed violently, struggling to her knees.

She blinked — and realized the cavern was gone.

The corridor they had entered through was gone.

Everything was gone, swallowed by water and light.

She turned.
Chrissy lay beside her, groaning but alive.

Above them, a soft golden light filtered down — daylight.

The reservoir had cracked open.

They were safe.

Aya clutched the remains of the locket in her hand — a single, broken chain now — and smiled through her tears.

It was over.
The bloodline's curse was broken.

The Forgotten were free.

And for the first time in generations... so was she.

Hours Later. They sat on the grassy bank, wrapped in blankets given by the first responders.
Apparently, someone had called 911 after hearing a massive explosion from the woods.

Chrissy nudged Aya gently. "You did it, you know."

Aya stared out over the ruined reservoir, the water churning where the cavern had collapsed.
The mist was gone.
The air smelled clean.

"I didn't think I could," she admitted softly.

"But you did," Chrissy said. "You broke the cycle."

Aya closed her eyes, feeling the weight lift from her shoulders. Her ancestors — all those who had suffered — were finally at peace.

And she was finally free to live her own life. Not bound by blood. Not bound by fear.

But bound only by the choices she made — starting now.

[End of Chapter 22.]

CHAPTER TWENTY-THREE

The First Binding

The storm raged over the thick Mississippi woods, lightning clawing across the sky like the hands of angry spirits. The year was 1837, and deep within a hidden glen, a secret gathering of souls began their rituals under the heavy cover of night. This was a place where the land could still remember its ancient origins, a place where magic had not yet been silenced by time.

Eunice LaRoux, a woman of regal yet untamed presence, stood at the center of a crude stone circle, her skin gleaming with the sheen of perspiration in the flickering torchlight. Her eyes, dark as midnight, reflected the intensity of the storm as she raised her hands, signaling the group to fall into a hush. A dozen others surrounded her — men and women of mixed heritage, born free and bound alike. Farmers, craftsmen, and those who had fled the chains of slavery in search of sanctuary. They were the keepers of forgotten knowledge, the guardians of old truths.

Tonight, they would make the ultimate sacrifice, bound by a destiny none of them could truly understand.

"Bring the vessel!" Eunice commanded, her voice commanding the wind to listen.

A man stepped forward from the circle, cradling a simple, cracked clay jar. It was unassuming, but within it was a darkness older than the river that ran through the land, darker than the earth that now trembled beneath their feet. This jar contained the essence of Vaylen, a spirit long feared, a malevolent force whose hunger for souls had ravaged the land for centuries. No one knew its true origins, only that it was something other — neither man nor beast, but a dark entity that feasted on the misery of humanity.

"Place it in the center," Eunice said softly, her voice trembling but resolute. The man complied, carefully setting the jar down before her.

Eunice bent low, brushing her fingers over the top of the jar as if trying to calm the beast that stirred inside. Her mother had warned her of this day — this moment when she would face the spirit, and in facing it, make a decision that would ripple through the generations.

Her hands shook as she reached for the jar, its warmth unnerving. A bead of sweat trickled down her neck, and the air seemed to grow heavier with each passing second. Her ancestors had whispered of such rituals, but none had truly believed the consequences would be as severe as they feared. But it was too late for hesitation now.

"Bind it, Eunice," a woman's voice urged from the circle. "We cannot let it roam free again."

Eunice nodded, her mind a whirlwind of conflicting emotions. She had always known there would be a price to pay for their protection, a price for controlling the chaos within their bloodline.

"Hold steady," she murmured to herself as she drew a deep breath. Then, with a steadying hand, she began to speak words taught to her by her own mother, and her mother before that. Words forbidden, words ancient, words spoken in a tongue older than any known language. They were words that had the power to both create and destroy.

The ground beneath her began to tremble as if the earth itself were alive and resisting. But Eunice did not flinch. The chant built in power as the others joined in, their voices rising in unison until they were one, connected in purpose.

A sickening crack echoed through the forest as the earth opened beneath the jar, a deep rift spreading outward like the jaws of a beast about to consume them all. Eunice's breath quickened, but she held firm, focusing on the words, her hand still pressing against the clay. The force within the jar began to pulse, as if the spirit was fighting back, desperate for freedom.

Eunice's bloodied palm met the cold earth, and she felt the pulse beneath her fingertips. This was the price — this was the bond that would tether her bloodline to Vaylen forever. But even as she sealed the spirit beneath the earth, she knew this would not be the last time the curse would reach for her descendants. They would bear this burden, generation after generation, until the very end.

When the final chant was uttered, the earth closed over the jar, sealing it deep within the soil. The rift vanished, leaving only the sound of the storm as it raged above. Eunice's body trembled, her face pale as death itself. She had done it. She had bound Vaylen to her bloodline, knowing full well that she and her descendants would carry both its protection and its curse.

But as the storm began to subside, Eunice felt a chill run down her spine, one that had nothing to do with the weather. She turned, looking over her shoulder at the man who had handed her the jar. His face was pale, his eyes wide with fear.

"We are not safe, Eunice," he whispered. "The spirit... it is not fully gone. It is waiting."

She nodded slowly, her heart sinking with the weight of the truth. The curse was not over. It had only just begun.

Present Day

Aya awoke with a start, her breath sharp and ragged. The dream — or rather, the vision — had felt all too real. She could still smell the sharp sting of ash and earth, the crackling of the storm in the distance. Eunice's face, filled with determination and terror, haunted her mind. And most terrifying of all, she could still feel the pull of something dark within her, tugging at her very soul.

"Aya? You okay?" Chrissy's voice was a whisper from across the room. Her gaze was fixed on Aya, a mix of concern and confusion written across her face.

Aya's heart pounded in her chest as she slowly sat up, trying to shake off the remnants of the vision. She could still feel the power of the spirit, the darkness that had been bound to her bloodline.

"It wasn't just a dream," Aya whispered hoarsely. "It was real. The curse... it's not gone. It's still waiting."

Chrissy's eyes widened. She had heard the legends — the stories passed down from those who knew the old ways. But seeing it in Aya's eyes now was a different matter entirely.

"Aya," Chrissy began, her voice tinged with urgency. "We need to find out more about this. The bloodline... the curse... I don't think it's done with us."

Aya nodded grimly. "No, it's far from over. And we're not safe yet."

[End of Chapter 23.]

CHAPTER TWENTY-FOUR

Echoes in the Bloodline

Aya couldn't shake the feeling that something was wrong. The air was heavy with the weight of her dreams—or perhaps they were visions—and the knowledge that the curse of Vaylen still clung to her bloodline. As much as she tried to convince herself that it was all a product of her overactive imagination, there was a chill in the air that felt like a warning.

She stood by the window of her apartment, staring out at the city streets below. The rhythmic hum of life outside seemed so distant compared to the turmoil stirring inside her. The weight of her newfound responsibility, the knowledge of the bloodline that bound her to this ancient curse, felt suffocating. She wasn't just running from Vaylen anymore; she was running from a legacy that had been written long before her birth.

It had been a week since the vision of Eunice LaRoux, and Aya couldn't help but feel as if she were caught in a trap of her own making. Her mind kept returning to the haunting words from her dream. The curse is not over. It is waiting.

"Aya, you've been quiet," Chrissy's voice interrupted her thoughts as she entered the room, her eyes narrowing with concern. "You haven't been sleeping, have you?"

Aya shook her head, but the lie felt hollow in her throat. "I'm fine," she said, her voice steady but lacking its usual conviction.

Chrissy wasn't fooled. "Talk to me. What's going on? This... this thing with the curse, the bloodline... you can't carry that burden alone."

Aya turned to face her best friend, the one person who had stood by her through every twisted turn of this journey. Chrissy had become more than just a friend; she was a sister, someone who saw through the layers of Aya's facade.

"I don't know what's real anymore," Aya admitted, her voice raw. "The visions I've been having, they feel too real. It's like I'm reliving what Eunice went through, but... it's mine now. It's my curse. And I can't escape it."

Chrissy stepped closer, her hand resting gently on Aya's shoulder. "Then we'll face it together. We don't know everything, but we can start digging deeper. We can figure out what's happening to you, Aya. You don't have to do this alone."

Aya looked into Chrissy's eyes, seeing the determination and love there. It was the same love that had pulled her from the brink of despair in the past, and it was the only thing that seemed to give her any hope now. But even with Chrissy by her side, Aya knew the path ahead was treacherous.

"We need to go back," Aya said suddenly, the thought forming fully in her mind. "We need to go back to the place where I found the journal—the one that's been guiding me. Maybe there's more there, something we missed."

Chrissy hesitated for a moment, uncertainty flickering in her eyes. "The ruins? That's dangerous, Aya. We don't know what we're dealing with. What if—"

"We don't have a choice," Aya interrupted. Her voice had taken on a fiercer edge, the weight of the curse pushing her forward. "If this is going to end, it has to end there. We need to find out what really happened to Eunice and the others."

The drive to the old ruins felt like a pilgrimage, each mile bringing them closer to the answers they both needed but feared. The landscape around them was desolate, the remnants of long-abandoned homes and broken-down shacks dotting the otherwise empty stretch of land. The closer they got, the more Aya's unease grew.

"We don't even know what we're going to find," Chrissy said, her voice tense as she glanced at Aya. "What if it's worse than we think?"

Aya swallowed hard, her gaze fixed straight ahead. "We don't know anything for sure. But the journal, the visions… they're all pointing here. This is where it all started, and it's where it's going to end."

As they arrived at the ruins, the air grew thick with the same oppressive energy that had filled the forest in her vision. The ruins, long abandoned by those who once lived there, now stood as a testament to the past—a place where the earth itself seemed to remember the dark rituals that had taken place within its soil.

Aya took a deep breath as she stepped out of the car, the weight of the moment pressing down on her shoulders. "Stay close," she instructed, her voice low but commanding. "And be ready for anything."

Together, they made their way through the overgrown path leading into the heart of the ruins. The air was thick with a palpable sense of dread, the kind that made Aya's skin crawl and her heart race. It was as if the very ground beneath her feet was aware of her presence, like it was waiting for something.

As they reached the center of the ruins, Aya's eyes landed on the same stone circle from her vision. The memory of the ritual—the binding of Vaylen to the LaRoux bloodline—flashed through her mind like a movie on rewind. The power of the spirit, the dark magic that had been unleashed… it was all still there, waiting.

"We're here," Aya whispered, her breath catching in her throat.

Suddenly, the ground beneath them rumbled. The earth trembled as if something was awakening deep beneath their feet. Aya's heart skipped a beat as she turned to Chrissy, who looked just as alarmed.

"I don't think we're alone," Chrissy said, her voice shaking.

Aya nodded grimly. "I think the curse is finally catching up to us."

The air around them seemed to crackle with energy as the ground trembled again, louder this time. Something ancient, something powerful, was stirring in the depths of the earth—and Aya knew, deep in her bones, that it was coming for them.

The echoes of the past were closing in.

[End of Chapter 24.]

CHAPTER TWENTY-FIVE

The Awakening

The rumble beneath their feet was no longer just a tremor—it was a growl, deep and primal, reverberating through the air around them. Aya's heart pounded in her chest, each beat louder than the last. The earth seemed to open beneath them, a crack forming in the ground where the stone circle once stood, as if the very earth itself was remembering the ancient ritual that had been performed here.

"Aya... we need to leave, now," Chrissy's voice was urgent, but Aya could feel the pull of the place, as if something was calling her to stay.

"No. We have to stay. We have to finish this," Aya responded, her words firm despite the rising fear in her voice. Her eyes locked onto the crack in the earth, the widening fissure that seemed to beckon her forward. It was like it had been waiting for her—waiting for the bloodline to return.

Chrissy hesitated, fear flickering in her eyes, but she stepped forward, her hand gripping Aya's arm. "I don't know if we can do this alone, Aya. What if we're not meant to stop it?"

Aya's grip tightened on the stone of the circle, as the tremors increased. "We don't have a choice. We're already in this. The curse—it's been passed down through generations. The only way to end it is to confront it."

The air around them shifted, heavy with dark energy. The temperature dropped, their breath forming visible clouds in the cold atmosphere. A deep, resonant voice boomed from the very depths of the earth, as though the ruins themselves were speaking. "Bloodline... return to me."

Aya felt the voice in her chest, vibrating through her bones. It wasn't a voice she could hear with her ears, but one she felt deep inside her. It was an ancient, malevolent presence— something that had been waiting, dormant for centuries, until her bloodline finally returned to stir it awake.

"Vaylen," she whispered, the name tasting like ash on her tongue. "This is it."

Chrissy's grip on her arm tightened. "What is that thing? It's—it's real. It's not just some ghost from the past. It's alive."

Aya nodded slowly, her heart pounding with an overwhelming mix of fear and determination. The curse was not just some legend. It was a living, breathing force that had been bound to her ancestors, and now it had found its way back to her. The bloodline—the very thing she had tried to escape—was now the key to ending the nightmare.

"Look at the circle," Aya murmured, staring at the shifting stone, the cracks widening and forming into intricate symbols that seemed to pulse with dark energy. "It's a gateway. The ritual wasn't just binding the bloodline—it was sealing something away."

She stepped closer to the crack in the earth, her foot hovering above the fissure. The ground was unstable, trembling as if something far more powerful than any storm was stirring beneath their feet.

"Whatever we do, we can't let it open fully," Aya said, her voice firm. "We have to stop it."

Chrissy was shaking, her fear evident, but her resolve matched Aya's. "Then what do we do? We don't even know what we're up against."

Aya hesitated, feeling the weight of her family's curse bearing down on her. She thought back to the journal—the one piece of the puzzle that had always guided her. In it, Eunice LaRoux had written about the ancient ritual, about the curse, and the bloodline. There had to be a way to reverse it, to stop whatever dark force was waiting below.

Suddenly, the ground trembled again, the fissure expanding rapidly. The cold wind picked up, swirling around them like a storm had been conjured just for their arrival. A flash of blinding light erupted from the crack, and in that moment, Aya saw it—the form of a figure rising from the depths.

It was a figure cloaked in shadow, its features distorted and twisted, as if it had been waiting in the darkness for centuries to rise again. The presence was suffocating, and Aya could feel it pulling at her, trying to invade her mind, to make her bend to its will.

"Vaylen!" Aya shouted, stepping forward, her fists clenched at her sides. "I'm not afraid of you!"

The shadowed figure paused, its distorted face locking eyes with hers. Aya felt the immense power radiating from it, the oppressive force of its ancient magic pressing against her, but she stood her ground.

"You think you can stop me, child of the bloodline?" The voice was like the sound of a thousand whispers, a chilling, malevolent hiss. "You are nothing but a vessel—a tool. The curse will not end. It will live on through you, just as it has through your ancestors."

Aya's pulse quickened, but she didn't flinch. "I won't let you use me anymore. The bloodline ends with me."

With that declaration, Aya reached deep within herself, tapping into a power she had never fully understood until now. The bloodline had always been a curse, but it was also a part of her—a part that could be wielded, controlled. She could feel the magic coursing through her veins, ancient and raw, and for the first time, she knew exactly what to do.

With a cry of determination, she released the energy, sending a wave of brilliant, blinding light toward the shadowy figure. It recoiled, its form flickering and distorting in the face of her power. For the first time, Aya could see it weakening, losing its grip on the world.

But it wasn't enough. The creature—the spirit—was too powerful, its grip too strong. Aya could feel it pushing back, trying to claw its way back into the physical realm.

"Aya, we need to finish this!" Chrissy's voice broke through the chaos, but it was faint, as though she were speaking from a distance.

Aya's focus wavered for a moment, but she couldn't allow herself to falter. The curse would end now, or it would never end at all.

She focused all her energy into one final, devastating strike. With a guttural cry, she unleashed everything she had, forcing the shadow back into the depths. The ground trembled once more, but this time, the fissure closed, sealing the creature away.

For a moment, everything was still. The air was thick with the aftermath, the silence deafening.

"Is it over?" Chrissy's voice was trembling as she stepped closer, her face pale.

Aya looked around the ruined circle, the oppressive energy gone. The storm of darkness had passed, and for the first time, she felt a sense of relief. She nodded slowly.

"I think it's over," she said, her voice hoarse.

But deep in her soul, Aya knew that the battle wasn't truly finished. The bloodline would always be a part of her, and while this chapter had closed, there was still more to learn, more to uncover about the curse—and about herself.

The echoes of the bloodline had quieted, but they would never fully fade.

[End of Chapter 25.]

CHAPTER TWENTY-SIX

The Unbroken Circle

The days following the destruction of the shadow were filled with silence, a heavy kind of quiet that settled over Aya and Chrissy like a weight they couldn't shake. They had gone back to the house, to the remnants of the circle, where the earth was now still, and the stones no longer pulsed with dark energy. It felt like a finality, a closure they hadn't expected.

But Aya couldn't ignore the unease that crept into her bones. There was something left unsaid, something unaccounted for. The curse had been sealed—but not defeated.

It had been too easy.

They were in Chrissy's apartment now, and Aya stared out the window at the darkened streets below, her mind racing. Chrissy, who had been pacing nervously, finally sat down beside her.

"You're still thinking about it, aren't you?" Chrissy's voice was soft, but the tension in it was undeniable. "About what happened at the circle... It can't just be over, right? I mean, it's too quiet."

Aya glanced over at her friend, her eyes heavy. "I keep feeling like it's watching me. The bloodline. It's like it's waiting for something. But I don't know what."

"It's not just you," Chrissy replied, her voice tight. "I keep seeing things—shadows moving where they shouldn't. And I swear I hear whispers when I'm alone. It's almost like it's trying to come back. But why now? I thought we sealed it. I thought we—"

"I know," Aya interrupted, her voice barely above a whisper. "But what if it's not gone? What if it's still inside of me? What if it's never really gone?" Her fingers trembled as they traced the edge of the journal on the table in front of them—the journal that had started it all.

The journal was an ancient relic, passed down from one LaRoux to the next. It had been filled with warnings, rituals, history—things they had never truly understood until now. Now, it felt heavier than ever, like the weight of generations pressing down on her.

"There's got to be a way to stop it," Aya muttered, more to herself than to Chrissy.

"I hope so." Chrissy's tone was hesitant, but there was something else beneath the fear—determination. She wouldn't give up now. Neither of them would.

Aya took a deep breath. "I'm going to find the answers. There's more to this curse than just what we saw in that circle. The bloodline has to have a weakness. I just have to figure out what it is."

Chrissy looked at her, a concerned frown on her face. "But how do you do that? You've already seen everything in that journal. You've already faced the worst of it."

Aya stood up, her legs stiff. "There's always more. I know there is. And I need to learn it before it's too late."

Without another word, Aya walked to the door. She wasn't sure what she was looking for, but the compulsion to keep searching was overwhelming. Whatever this curse was, whatever the bloodline truly held, she couldn't stop until she uncovered it all.

"I'm going to the library," she said over her shoulder. "I need to see if there's more about this—more about the LaRoux bloodline. If I can understand it better, maybe I can finally stop it."

"But what if it's a trap?" Chrissy called out. "What if you're just digging yourself deeper?"

Aya hesitated for a moment, then turned to face Chrissy. "I don't know, but I can't just sit here and wait for it to come back. I need to know what we're really up against."

The library was quiet, a place of dust and forgotten history. Aya had always felt a strange connection to it, a pull that had been with her since she was young. Now, it felt like a sanctuary—or perhaps a tomb. She didn't know which.

The moment she stepped through the door, the familiar scent of old books filled her nose. It wasn't the smell of the books themselves—those had become familiar over time. It was something else, something older, something that whispered from the pages that lined the shelves.

Aya wandered through the rows, not sure where she was going. Her footsteps echoed in the silence, and she felt more and more like an intruder, like she didn't belong here anymore.

The whole place seemed to hum with ancient energy.

Finally, her feet led her to a secluded corner of the library, where an old wooden table stood. Upon it, there was an open book—one she hadn't noticed before.

She picked it up, the dust sliding off the cover. The book was smaller than most, its pages worn, and the ink faded. But the moment she opened it, a chill ran through her.

The book was a history of the LaRoux family, yes—but it was more than that. This was a record of the family's rituals, their ties to the ancient forces they had tried to escape, and their continued involvement in powers far beyond mortal comprehension.

The last page was what caught her attention. It had a name on it, but it wasn't a LaRoux name—it was Vaylen.

Her heart skipped a beat as she read the text.

"Vaylen, a being bound by blood, seeks to re-enter the world. His return will bring devastation unless the bloodline fulfills its final purpose. One shall bind him, the other shall break him. But beware, for the choice is not only of blood—but of will. Only when the bloodline is broken, when its power is severed, shall Vaylen truly be stopped."

Aya's breath caught in her throat as she realized what this meant. There was more to the curse than just defeating the shadow. The bloodline could break, could sever the tie to Vaylen—but it would take an unimaginable sacrifice.

Could she do it? Could she end the curse once and for all?

[End of Chapter 26.]

CHAPTER TWENTY-SEVEN

The Hidden Passage

The full moon's glow barely pierced through the boarded windows of the LaRoux estate. Dust floated thick in the air, swirling like spirits disturbed from slumber. Chrissy coughed into her sleeve, squinting at the ancient floorboards Aya was examining with her pocket flashlight.

"You sure it's here?" Chrissy whispered, her voice quivering.

Aya didn't answer immediately. Her fingers traced the symbols carved faintly into the wood — the same markings they'd found in her great-grandmother's diary. They matched perfectly. She pressed one palm flat against the largest carving, feeling a vibration hum against her skin.

The floor gave a low groan.

Then — with a shuddering breath of stale air — a portion of the floorboards shifted, revealing a staircase spiraling down into darkness.

Chrissy backed away instinctively. "Nope. Nope, absolutely not. That looks like straight-up demon nonsense."

Aya gave her a tight, trembling smile. "If the answers are down there, we don't have a choice."

They stared at the yawning maw of the hidden passage for a long, heart-thudding moment. The air that wafted up was colder than anything above — damp, metallic, and thick with the scent of earth long undisturbed.

Aya took the first step.

Each footfall creaked against stone steps worn smooth by time. Chrissy hesitated, muttering prayers under her breath, then followed closely, clutching Aya's sleeve. The flashlight's beam flickered against the walls, revealing murals painted in blood-red pigments: scenes of rituals, shadowy figures in masks, and a tree — gnarled and black — standing atop a pile of bones.

"I hate this," Chrissy hissed, her fingers tightening painfully on Aya's arm.

Aya swallowed her fear. "Stay close."

The staircase ended in a vast underground hall. Columns of cracked stone stretched into the darkness. Strange sounds echoed — whispers that seemed to come from nowhere. Their footsteps stirred the dust into frantic spirals around their ankles.

In the center of the hall stood an altar.

Upon it, a heavy book rested — its cover bound in something that looked disturbingly like skin.

Aya stepped forward, her heart hammering. As she approached, the whispering grew louder, as if the very walls breathed secrets. She touched the book's surface — and the world around them shifted.

The ground trembled.

Chrissy screamed as the walls began to ripple like water. The murals peeled themselves from the stone and moved, figures stepping free from the rock, ghostly and silent. Spectral ancestors — guardians of the bloodline — now watching, judging.

"Aya!" Chrissy cried, grabbing her arm.

The altar cracked open like an egg, and from within rose a figure — a woman draped in tattered robes, her eyes glowing with a sickly green fire.

"Descendants," the woman rasped, her voice like the rustling of dead leaves. "You awaken what should have remained sealed."

Aya forced herself to stand her ground. "Who are you?"

The woman's head tilted at an unnatural angle. "I am the First Warden. Bound to protect the Bloodroot... and punish the unworthy."

The temperature plummeted. Frost bloomed across the floor in delicate spiderweb patterns. The specters circled closer, murmuring ancient words.

Chrissy pulled Aya back. "We need to go, now."

But there was nowhere to run.

The stone columns shifted again — forming a labyrinth around them. The specters began to chase, shrieking in distorted voices. Aya grabbed Chrissy's hand, dragging her through the twisting passages. Every turn seemed to lead deeper into the underground maze.

"This way!" Aya gasped, spotting a narrow tunnel ahead.

They darted inside, sliding down a slope of loose gravel. Behind them, the First Warden's voice thundered through the halls:

"You cannot escape the Bloodline's Judgment!"

They stumbled into a smaller chamber, gasping for breath. Strange crystals embedded in the walls pulsed with eerie red light. In the center, another mural — this one depicting two girls standing before the black tree, offering a piece of themselves.

Chrissy collapsed against the wall. "I—I can't... I can't do this."

Aya knelt beside her, gripping her shoulders. "Listen to me — we're not going to die here. We were meant to find this place. There's something they don't want us to know."

"But what if..." Chrissy's voice broke. "What if we are the sacrifice?"

Aya looked up at the mural again.

The black tree loomed larger, its twisted branches reaching for them like claws. But in the mural's corner — almost hidden — was a symbol they hadn't seen before: a door. A way out.

Aya's mind raced.

"This isn't just a tomb," she realized aloud. "It's a test."

Chrissy wiped her tears. "What do we have to do?"

Aya studied the mural carefully. "We have to confront it — the heart of the curse. That's the only way out."

Another tremor shook the ground.

The First Warden's ghostly form seeped through the walls, howling like a winter storm.

They had no more time to hesitate.

Aya grabbed Chrissy's hand, determination hardening in her chest. "Let's end this," she said.

Together, they plunged deeper into the unknown.

[End of Chapter 27.]

CHAPTER TWENTY-EIGHT

The Forgotten Secret

Aya and Chrissy stepped cautiously into the dimly lit passage, the air damp and cool against their skin. The narrow walls pressed in on them, and the faint smell of old earth and stone filled the air. Each step they took seemed to echo louder in the silence, making it feel like the whole house was holding its breath. The flickering light from their lanterns cast strange shadows on the walls, adding to the eerie atmosphere.

The passage seemed to stretch on forever. Aya's mind raced, her heart pounding in her chest. She had known this house was full of secrets, but nothing could have prepared her for this—this hidden world beneath the surface. She glanced at Chrissy, who was just a few paces behind, her face tense with a mix of excitement and fear.

"Do you think anyone else has been down here?" Chrissy whispered, her voice barely audible over the sound of their footsteps.

"I don't know," Aya replied, her eyes scanning the dark passage ahead. "But it doesn't feel... natural. Like it's been waiting for us to find it."

As they ventured deeper into the tunnel, a faint glow began to emerge from the walls. It wasn't from their lanterns, but something older, something imbued into the very stone. The light seemed to pulse with an otherworldly energy, casting eerie, dancing shadows across the path before them. Aya felt the hair on the back of her neck stand up as she continued forward, each step more deliberate, her senses heightened.

"What is that?" Chrissy muttered, her voice filled with awe. "It's like the walls are alive."

Aya didn't respond. She was too transfixed by the glow. Something—something ancient and powerful—was calling to her, and she couldn't explain why, but she felt that they were close to something important.

Soon, they reached the heart of the passage. The tunnel opened up into a small, circular chamber. In the center stood a pedestal, the stone smooth and worn with age.

The glow emanated from a small object resting atop the pedestal, illuminating the chamber with a soft, ethereal light. Aya felt a shiver of anticipation run through her as she moved closer.

On the pedestal lay a small box, no larger than the size of her palm. The box was intricately carved with strange symbols— some she recognized, others that were completely foreign. The carvings seemed to shift and move when she looked closely, like the symbols were alive and reacting to her presence.

"What is that?" Chrissy breathed, taking a cautious step forward.

"I don't know," Aya replied, her voice thick with wonder. She reached out instinctively, her fingers brushing the cold surface of the box. The moment she touched it, a strange pulse of energy coursed through her fingertips, as though the box were alive, responding to her touch.

Aya recoiled, startled by the sudden surge of power. She took a step back, her heart racing. Something wasn't right. She could feel the power emanating from the box, a dark and ancient energy, like a living thing waiting to be awakened.

"It feels... wrong," Aya muttered.

"Do you think it's safe?" Chrissy asked, her eyes wide with unease.

Aya's gaze was fixed on the box. She could sense that it wasn't just a relic or a forgotten trinket—it was something far more dangerous. Something that had been hidden away for a reason.

"I don't know," she replied softly, still too afraid to touch it again.

Just as she was about to turn away, a low, rumbling sound echoed through the chamber, vibrating in her chest. The walls seemed to tremble, and the air grew thick with tension. Aya's breath hitched. "Did you hear that?" she whispered.

Before Chrissy could respond, the temperature in the chamber plummeted. A cold wind swept through the room, though there were no windows or doors. The strange glow from the box blazed brighter, casting flickering shadows on the walls.

"I think we need to leave," Aya said urgently, backing toward the entrance. But as she moved, the ground beneath her feet began to shift. The stone floor groaned and cracked, like something deep within the earth was waking up.

"Aya!" Chrissy cried, her voice tinged with panic. "What's happening?"

"I don't know!" Aya yelled back, her voice barely cutting through the roar of the shaking passage. The air around them seemed to crackle with energy. The walls started to close in, the stone shifting like it was alive, pressing them toward the center of the room. The pedestal with the box remained untouched, though the light from it had become blinding.

Suddenly, the voice came—low and commanding, like a rumble of thunder in the distance, but it was unmistakably close. "You've awoken me."

Aya froze. Her heart slammed in her chest. The voice wasn't coming from any living thing—it was coming from the box, from the power within it. The sound reverberated through the chamber, filling her mind with an eerie sense of inevitability. It was like the box had been waiting for her all this time.

"Aya, we need to get out now!" Chrissy shouted, her face pale with fear.

Aya's instincts kicked in, and she grabbed Chrissy's hand, pulling her toward the exit. But the tunnel had changed. The walls now seemed to stretch and warp, twisting into a labyrinth of shadows. The once-straight path had become a maze of impossible angles and turns.

"Run!" Aya screamed, her pulse pounding in her ears. They had to get out, and fast. But the tunnel seemed to close in on them with every step, pushing them further into its depths. It was like the house itself was alive, trapping them inside.

As they stumbled through the maze of shifting walls, Aya glanced back. The glow from the box had dimmed, but the air was still thick with the presence of something ancient and powerful. Something that had been waiting for them.

"We can't stop!" Aya cried, tugging Chrissy faster.

Just as they reached what seemed to be a dead end, the tunnel trembled again, the ground shaking violently. And then, in the distance, the faintest glimmer of light—real light—shone through a crack in the stone. They ran toward it, bursting through the narrow opening, gasping for air as they tumbled into the yard outside.

They collapsed on the ground, panting and shaking from the ordeal. Aya's heart still raced, and her skin was cold with sweat. She looked back at the house, the dark silhouette looming behind them.

"We... we have to go back," Aya whispered, the realization settling in. "We've unleashed something. And it's not over yet."

[End of Chapter 28.]

CHAPTER TWENTY-NINE

Veil of Whispers

The woods behind the Holloway house seemed endless under the thick, black night. Aya clutched Chrissy's hand tighter as they moved carefully along the narrow, twisted path that had revealed itself after the last ritual. The air was damp and electric, like a storm was waiting just above their heads, unseen but heavy.

Every branch they brushed past seemed to whisper in a voice just out of reach. And though no one was behind them, they both kept looking back.

"We shouldn't be here," Chrissy said in a harsh whisper, her eyes wide and flickering with panic. "That old journal said the Veil is thinnest tonight. If something's hiding between the worlds—"

"We don't have a choice," Aya cut in. "It's the only way to find the real source. We're running out of time."

She hated how unsteady her voice sounded. Inside, she felt just as terrified. But she had to lead. She had to pretend she wasn't drowning in fear.

The deeper they went, the more unnatural the woods became.
The trees grew too close together, their trunks twisting around each other like living things trying to strangle the sky. Small orbs of cold blue light floated in the distance — sometimes blinking out when looked at directly.

Aya noticed the scent then — something sour and metallic, clinging to the air.
Blood.
Old blood.

They stopped at a clearing where the ground sagged downward, forming a natural bowl. At the center, a large standing stone pierced upward, cracked with time, covered in carvings that seemed to shimmer.

"It's the Veil Stone," Chrissy whispered. "This is it."

Before Aya could respond, the ground beneath their feet shifted slightly.
A rumble — so faint they almost missed it.
Then, slowly, a slit opened in the ground near

the stone, revealing steps descending into
darkness.

Aya's heart slammed against her ribs. She
thought about the warning scrawled in the
margins of the journal:

"Once opened, the path demands a
price."

But what other choice did they have?

Aya swallowed her fear.
Chrissy gave her a tiny nod, just as pale and
determined.
Together, they descended into the hidden
earth.

The temperature dropped instantly.
The walls were stone but slick with moisture.
Faint markings—symbols Aya recognized
from the Holloway sigil—glowed softly along
the way.

The whispers grew louder here. Now
they could hear bits and pieces:

"Sins buried... blood remembered...
awaken..."

At the bottom of the stairs, the tunnel
opened into a cavernous underground
chamber.

Bones lined the walls — hundreds of them.
Some human, some... not quite.
And at the center, a stone dais.
A black book rested atop it, pulsing like a
beating heart.

Chrissy clutched Aya's arm.

"This is blood magic," she said, barely
able to get the words out. "Deep magic. The
kind no one's supposed to ever find."

Aya stepped forward despite herself.
The book called to her — not with words, but
a feeling, an echo inside her blood.

As she reached out, the ground
shuddered again.
Shapes began to rise from the bone piles —
twisting, half-formed creatures with hollow
eyes.

The guardians of the secret.

Aya yanked Chrissy back just in time as
the first one lunged.

They sprinted for the stairs, but the
tunnel seemed longer now, distorted by some
dark force.

The creatures followed, shrieking in voices that weren't quite human. Their wails scraped against the mind.

Aya remembered something — something she read.

"They cannot leave the chamber. They are bound to the blood grounds." They just had to make it out.

Gasping, heart pounding, she and Chrissy burst from the tunnel just as the creatures slammed into an invisible wall at the entrance, howling in fury.

They collapsed in the clearing, staring back at the stone.

And then, Aya realized she was still clutching the black book.

It had let her take it.
Which meant...
It wanted to be found.

Above them, the sky split with a crack of lightning, illuminating a figure standing at the tree line — cloaked, watching.

Not all guardians were trapped below.

[End of Chapter 29.]

CHAPTER THIRTY

The Cloaked One

The rain came hard and sudden,
pounding the clearing in icy sheets. Aya and
Chrissy scrambled to their feet, the black
book tucked firmly under Aya's arm.
But they weren't looking at the storm.

Their eyes were locked on the figure
standing just beyond the edge of the trees.

Tall. Cloaked. Motionless.

Aya couldn't see a face — just the shape
of someone watching them with unsettling
stillness.
For a moment, no one moved. The only
sounds were the rush of rain and the dying
echoes of the shrieking things below.

Chrissy gripped Aya's sleeve.

"Do we run?" she whispered.

Aya didn't answer. Something about the
figure held her in place — not with fear, but
with recognition. Like a half-remembered
dream.

The figure stepped forward.

Chrissy tensed, but Aya stayed still, her breath misting in the cold air.
The figure slowly raised a hand, palm open, revealing an object clutched in their fingers — a pendant, glinting silver and red under the flashes of lightning.

The Holloway crest.

Aya's mouth went dry.

Before she could react, the figure tossed the pendant onto the ground between them. It landed with a soft clink, and then — without a word — the figure turned and melted into the forest, vanishing into the storm.

Chrissy darted forward and snatched the pendant.

"It's real," she breathed, holding it out.

The pendant was old, tarnished by time, but unmistakable: the crest of the Holloway bloodline intertwined with symbols Aya didn't recognize — symbols matching the ones from the underground cavern.

Chrissy turned it over.

There was something carved into the back: a name.

"Arden Holloway."

"Another Holloway?" Chrissy asked, voice trembling. "But... we thought the line ended generations ago. There's no Arden in the records."

Aya stared into the woods where the figure had disappeared, heart pounding with a thousand unspoken questions.

Who was Arden?
Why now?
And most importantly — why help them?

She felt the weight of the book under her arm, almost humming with energy.

"We need to get back," Aya said finally, her voice low. "Before they realize we have this."

Chrissy nodded, casting a last, nervous glance at the darkened trees.
Together, they slipped back into the winding paths toward town, clutching their new prize and an even deeper mystery.

Neither of them noticed the other figures stirring in the woods now — drawn to the sudden change in the bloodline's story.

The storm had awakened more than just old bones.
It had awakened the war for the Holloway legacy.

[End of Chapter 30.]

CHAPTER THIRTY-ONE

Witches Mark

The air was thick with unease as Aya and Chrissy walked back into town, the moon veiled behind clouds that moved like smoke across the sky. They hadn't spoken much since returning from the Holloway estate. Something unspoken clung to Aya, and Chrissy could sense it in the way her friend's eyes lingered too long on shadows and her fingers curled tightly around the edges of her sleeves.

By the time they reached Chrissy's house, the streetlamps were flickering. Aya paused at the doorstep, her breath catching.

"Chrissy," she whispered. "Something's wrong with me."

Chrissy turned, heart pounding. "What do you mean?"

Aya held out her wrist. The skin there glowed faintly beneath the surface — a deep violet sigil, pulsing like a heartbeat. It was a symbol they had seen etched into the

pendant found beneath the Holloway crypt —
a looped spiral surrounded by four crescents.

Chrissy gasped. "When did that happen?"

"This morning. After I touched the book
again. At first, it burned… now it's like it's a
part of me."

Before Chrissy could respond, the
temperature in the room dropped.

A low hum vibrated through the walls,
like chanting from some far-off place. The
lights cut out.

And then — a knock at the back door.

They froze.

Another knock.

Aya whispered, "Don't answer it."

But Chrissy, driven by something
between fear and instinct, stepped to the back
door and peeked through the curtain.

A woman stood there — cloaked in a
long, gray coat, her face half-hidden by a veil
of midnight hair. Her eyes were ancient. Not
old. Ancient.

"I'm here for the girl," she said, voice like gravel scraping stone.

Chrissy stepped back. "Who are you?"

The woman entered uninvited. The candles in the room sparked to life, flickering as if acknowledging her presence.

"I'm not your enemy," she said. "Not yet."

Aya stepped forward, hand trembling, wrist still glowing. "What's happening to me?"

The woman gave a small nod of respect. "You've been marked. The sigil of Holloway's last true heir. The bloodline doesn't die — it blooms."

Aya swallowed. "Why now?"

"The witching hour of your legacy has begun. The seal your ancestors tried to suppress is cracking. Your blood remembers what they wanted to forget."

Chrissy interrupted, stepping between them. "What do you want from her?"

"To warn you. The ritual has already started. You opened it. When you read from that book, when you walked through that house… you called it forward. The curse is no longer dormant — it's alive. And it is hungry."

Aya stepped back, voice shaking. "Then how do I stop it?"

The woman studied her. "You don't. You finish what your ancestors could not. Or this town dies with you."

A gust of wind blew through the room, extinguishing every flame.

When the lights flickered back on, the woman was gone.

Aya collapsed onto the floor, breath shallow. Chrissy knelt beside her.

"What do we do now?" she asked.

Aya looked at her glowing wrist, then at the window where the woman had vanished.

"We stop running," she said. "We finish this."

[End of Chapter 31.]

CHAPTER THIRTY-TWO

The Bloodline Trials

The night had already stretched long into the morning when Aya and Chrissy found themselves standing at the town's edge, the forest looming before them like a dark, waiting creature. The wind had picked up, swirling around them in eerie whispers. Aya could feel it — the restless energy, the pull of the bloodline, as though the earth itself was calling to her.

"You sure this is where the first Anchor is?" Chrissy's voice cut through the silence, but even she couldn't hide the uncertainty that seeped into her tone.

Aya nodded, though the doubt gnawed at her. "The woman said we had to find them. The Anchors are tied to the curse, to the Holloway lineage." She glanced down at the sigil on her wrist, now faintly glowing again. "If we don't stop it now, everything we've seen will just be the beginning."

Chrissy shivered. "Great. No pressure."

They moved deeper into the woods, their footsteps muffled by the thick carpet of fallen leaves. The trail ahead was marked by symbols carved into the trees, barely visible but there if you knew where to look. The same symbols that had adorned the pendant, the crypt — and now, Aya's wrist.

Every instinct told Aya to turn back. She didn't belong here, not in the thick shadows of this cursed forest. But she had no choice. The pull of the bloodline was too strong, and the sigil was like a beacon guiding her forward.

They reached a clearing, and Aya stopped dead in her tracks. Before them stood an old stone structure — half-collapsed, overtaken by ivy and moss, its jagged edges weathered by time. This was it.

"Is this… the Anchor?" Chrissy asked, awe in her voice.

Aya nodded. The stone doorway seemed to pulse with an unseen energy, drawing her closer. The symbols etched into the walls shimmered faintly as though waiting for something — or someone.

As they approached, the ground beneath their feet trembled. The air thickened, pressing down on Aya's chest as though the very atmosphere was alive.

"This doesn't feel right," Chrissy muttered, glancing around nervously. "Something's off about this place."

Aya ignored her, focusing on the doorway. The sigil on her wrist began to burn again, a heat that spread up her arm and into her chest. She felt the stirrings of power — ancient, raw, and unsettling.

The moment her hand touched the stone, the earth beneath them split with a deafening crack. A gust of wind swept through the clearing, lifting the leaves in a chaotic dance. From the cracks in the stone, shadows began to creep out, coiling like serpents.

"Aya—" Chrissy shouted, grabbing her arm, but it was too late.

With a rush of force, the ground beneath their feet gave way. The two girls were thrown into the dark, and the world went black.

Aya gasped as she landed hard on the ground. The impact knocked the breath from her lungs, and for a moment, she couldn't move. She lay there, panting, feeling the weight of something heavy pressing down on her chest. Slowly, she pushed herself up, her eyes adjusting to the dim light.

They were in a cavern — deep beneath the earth, surrounded by walls of smooth stone that seemed to pulse with energy, like the very rock was alive. The air was thick with the smell of damp earth and something ancient, something wrong.

"Chrissy?" Aya called, her voice echoing.

"I'm here!" Chrissy's voice came from behind her. She was standing, brushing dirt off her clothes. "This place... it feels like a trap."

Aya felt it too. The pull of something powerful was stronger here, suffocating, and it took everything she had not to back away. Her wrist burned hotter now, the sigil almost searing her skin.

"This is it," Aya whispered, the words tasting strange on her tongue. "This is the place the woman warned me about. The first Anchor."

Chrissy frowned. "Are you sure?"

Aya nodded, walking toward the center of the cavern where a large stone altar lay. It was ancient, covered in dust, but the same symbols were carved into its surface. It pulsed with a dark energy, drawing her closer.

"Aya, no," Chrissy said, grabbing her wrist. "This is wrong. We should go back—"

Before she could finish, the ground beneath them began to rumble again. The symbols on the altar glowed bright red, and the air grew heavy with power.

Aya's wrist flared in response, a sudden rush of energy coursing through her. The sigil was alive — and with it, the magic that had been sealed for centuries.

"It's calling me," Aya murmured. She didn't know why she said it, but she knew it was true. The bloodline, the curse, everything was pulling her in.

Suddenly, the shadows in the cavern shifted, taking form. Figures materialized from the darkness, their eyes glowing like embers. They were ancient spirits, trapped here by the Anchors. Guardians, protectors — and now, hunters.

Aya's heart raced. She reached for Chrissy. "We have to finish this. We can't leave without it."

The spirits closed in, their whispers filling the cavern. The temperature dropped, and Aya's breath turned to mist. But she stood her ground, the sigil burning hot on her wrist, urging her forward.

"Aya," Chrissy whispered. "We need a plan."

But Aya already knew. This was the trial — the first of many. She had to prove she was worthy to stop the curse, to break the seal. And she was ready to face whatever came next.

With one final deep breath, Aya stepped toward the altar, feeling the ancient power surge through her veins. The spirits closed in, and the trial had begun.

[End of Chapter 32.]

CHAPTER THIRTY-THREE

Echoes of the Past

The cavern pulsed with power as Aya took another step forward. The spirits swirled around her, murmuring in long-forgotten tongues. Each whisper clawed at her mind — fragments of pain, guilt, betrayal. The stories of those who had come before her. Of those who had failed.

Chrissy stood just behind her, frozen between fear and faith. "Aya… are you sure you can do this?"

"I don't know," Aya admitted. Her voice echoed through the chamber, uncertain but steady. "But I don't think I have a choice."

The altar before them trembled. A blinding light erupted from the sigil carved into its surface, flooding the cavern with spectral energy. The shadows retreated momentarily, exposing a circular seal embedded in the stone floor. Symbols spun around it in a perfect ring, shifting like clockwork gears.

Aya's sigil flared again. As it did, a beam of light shot from her wrist into the seal — activating it.

The stone circle cracked, then opened.

From its depths, a mist rolled out, followed by a flicker of something... human.

A figure stepped through.

She was tall, draped in long black robes that moved as though underwater. Her face was obscured by a veil of shadow, but her voice was unmistakable — Aya's grandmother, Maren Holloway.

Aya gasped. "No. You're dead."

"I was," the apparition replied. Her voice was smooth and calm, laced with ancient magic. "But so is the future, unless you survive this trial."

Chrissy backed up a step. "This is way past anything I signed up for..."

Aya's hands shook. "You knew? You knew all of this and never told me?"

"I tried to protect you," Maren said, stepping closer. "But blood remembers. And blood always calls."

The cavern shuddered. More figures rose from the mist — echoes of Aya's ancestors. Each one carried a fragment of the curse. A choice made. A betrayal hidden. A price paid.

Aya realized the trial wasn't a battle. It was a reckoning.

"You must walk through their memories," Maren said. "Only then can you understand the weight of the Holloway name — and decide if you will carry it... or bury it."

Aya took a deep breath and stepped onto the seal.

The world shifted.

Suddenly, she was no longer in the cavern. The air smelled of rain and smoke. She stood on cobblestones slick with blood.

A memory.

Before her was a girl who looked just like her — but dressed in turn-of-the-century clothing. She was crying, a locket clutched in her hand as flames devoured the house behind her.

A voice echoed through the air: "You let them die. You chose the power over the people. Just like all the rest."

Then the scene shifted.

Now Aya was in a courtroom, where another ancestor — this one male, angry and defiant — stood trial. "I did what I had to!" he shouted. "You don't understand! The darkness chose me!"

Again, the world changed.

She saw war. She saw betrayal. She saw a Holloway burning a sigil into the earth with the blood of someone she loved.

Every memory, every sin, was passed down like an heirloom.

Aya fell to her knees. "Why show me this?"

Maren's voice returned: "Because to defeat the curse, you must own it. Only then will you be strong enough to rewrite it."

Back in the cavern, Chrissy watched helplessly as Aya collapsed.

The spirits swirled, pausing — judging.

Aya's eyes flew open. Something had changed.

She rose to her feet, steadier now, the sigil on her wrist glowing brighter than ever before. She had faced the ghosts of her past — and survived.

"I'm not afraid of what came before," she said aloud. "Because I'm going to be the end of it."

The cavern trembled again — but this time, it was retreating. The spirits bowed their heads and began to dissolve, one by one.

The Anchor had accepted her.

As the last shadow vanished, a faint chime echoed through the cavern. A crack formed down the middle of the altar — and within it lay a relic: a black obsidian key, pulsing with the same energy as her sigil.

Aya reached for it, hand trembling.

One Anchor down. Two more to go.

But as they climbed from the cavern, the wind whispered a warning:

The second trial would not be so forgiving.

[End of Chapter 33.]

CHAPTER THIRTY-FOUR

The Second Seal

The key burned against Aya's skin.

Not in a painful way, but with a slow, pulsing thrum that matched her heartbeat. It was as if it had fused with her — whispering secrets meant only for Holloway blood. She tucked it away inside her jacket, but the pressure of it lingered like a presence.

The trek from the Anchor site to the next location was colder, darker. The sky, once overcast, now bled red at the edges. Trees along the trail to the second Anchor bent in unnatural ways, as if recoiling from what waited ahead.

Chrissy broke the silence. "That key... it changed something in you."

Aya didn't respond immediately. She could feel it too. Ever since the trial — the visions, the memories — something had nested deep inside her chest. Like her ancestors weren't just remembered... they were watching. Maybe even insideher.

They crested the hill where the second Anchor site had been marked in the cryptic map left behind by Agent Rowe. A forgotten cathedral stood, half-swallowed by the forest, its steeple cracked and tilting, as if pleading with the heavens. The symbol of the Holloway bloodline was carved above its rotten doors.

Aya stepped forward. "This is it."

The doors groaned open at her touch.

Inside, the cathedral was a ruin. Pews covered in vines. Windows shattered, stained glass littering the floor like colored tears. At the far end, the altar still stood — but behind it loomed a giant circular mirror, black as obsidian, ringed in silver glyphs.

Aya's sigil glowed in response.

"Mirror magic," Chrissy whispered. "Oh, that's never good..."

Suddenly, the doors slammed shut behind them.

The mirror pulsed. And then — it spoke.

"Aya Holloway… to face the future, you must fight your reflection."

Without warning, the mirror shimmered — and another figure stepped through.

It was Aya.

But not her.

This Aya wore black from head to toe. Her eyes were silver, her smile sharp and joyless. The sigil on her wrist was warped, pulsing with corrupted energy.

Chrissy gasped. "It's you, but if you'd… changed."

"No," the dark version said smoothly. "It's her… if she'd embraced what she really is."

Aya stepped forward. "I'm not you."

"Oh, but you are. I'm the version of you who stopped pretending. The one who accepted the truth: you don't need friends… or hope… or rules. You just need power."

She moved fast.

Too fast.

A blast of energy surged from the twisted sigil, throwing Aya across the cathedral floor.

Chrissy ran to her side. "Aya!"

"I'm fine," she groaned. "Stay back."

Aya rose, hands shaking, blood trickling from her temple.

The other her sneered. "You can't beat me, Aya. Because I know what you really want. You want control. You want revenge. You want to burn it all down — just like every Holloway before you."

Aya's heartbeat pounded in her ears.

For a split second… she almost agreed.

But then she looked at Chrissy — scared, loyal, still there. She thought of the people she'd helped along the way. The spirits she'd freed. The truths she'd unearthed, not for power, but to stop the pain.

"No," she said. "I want to break the curse. Not become it."

Aya lifted her hands. Her sigil surged — not red or silver, but white-hot light, born from choice, not blood.

The two forces collided.

Mirror and real.

Light and shadow.

The battle wasn't just physical — it was internal. Every strike carried a memory, every dodge a regret. They fought through the pews, through shards of glass and crumbling stone, until the mirror cracked with a scream.

Aya pinned her darker self against the altar.

"You're not real," she said through clenched teeth.

Dark Aya grinned. "Neither are your chances."

Aya drove her glowing palm into the reflection's chest — and with a blast of energy, the dark version shattered into a thousand shards of obsidian.

The mirror behind the altar burst.

The second seal was broken.

The silence that followed was immense.

Chrissy helped her up. "You okay?"

Aya wiped blood from her cheek and nodded. "Yeah. But that fight… wasn't just with her. That was with myself."

From the mirror's rubble, a second key emerged — smaller than the first, but colder. It hummed as she picked it up.

Two down. One to go.

But this time, no whisper warned her.

This time, the silence felt like it was waiting.

[End of Chapter 34.]

CHAPTER THIRTY-FIVE

The Whispering Ashes

The final key was colder than the first two.

Aya kept it in her pocket, wrapped in a silk cloth she found in Agent Rowe's pack. Something about it didn't want to be touched for long. Every time her skin brushed the metal, it sent flashes of flickering fire, screaming faces, and crumbling buildings through her mind.

She hadn't told Chrissy yet, but she hadn't slept since the second seal was broken.

Not really.

Her dreams had turned into a battlefield of cryptic voices and blurred faces—some she recognized from the Holloway journals, others she was sure hadn't even been born yet. Time felt like it was folding in on itself, pulling her deeper into something she was barely holding together.

They followed Rowe's last coordinates north through the thickest part of Ashenridge

Forest, where trees stood like twisted blackened skeletons. Years ago, a fire had devoured half this region, and nothing had ever grown back. Not grass. Not moss. Just ash, like the land had exhaled and never inhaled again.

The final Anchor was buried somewhere in this scorched graveyard.

And they weren't alone.

Chrissy knelt beside a scorched tree stump, fingers running across a series of runes burned into the bark. "These weren't here before," she said. "Someone's been ahead of us."

Aya's breath steamed in the cold air. "Or watching."

They moved carefully, the sky dimming earlier than usual. Twilight wrapped around the ruins like a shroud. Every step kicked up black dust. The forest was too quiet. Not even birds.

They reached a clearing.

At its center stood a massive black obelisk, broken at the top like it had been struck by lightning. Around it, six smaller stones formed a ring — each marked with a Holloway sigil. One for every generation. One for every blood sacrifice.

Chrissy exhaled. "This is it. This is the Final Anchor."

Aya stepped forward, the two keys humming in her pockets. The third—wrapped in silk—suddenly pulsed hot, even through the fabric.

Then the wind howled.

The ashes lifted off the ground.

They swirled like a storm — no longer dust, but shapes.

Figures.

Dozens of them.

Some were childlike. Others monstrous. All spectral. All whispering.

The spirits of those who'd died under the Holloway curse.

They didn't attack.

They circled.

Watching.

Judging.

One, a tall woman with a fire-scorched dress and hollow eyes, stepped forward.

"You broke two seals," she said. Her voice echoed like a forgotten prayer. "You think that makes you worthy?"

Aya swallowed. "No. But it makes me responsible."

The spirit tilted her head. "The Holloways made this place a graveyard."

"I know."

"They used us. Fed on our pain."

"I'm here to end that."

"Then prove it."

The obelisk split.

A stairwell spiraled downward beneath it, glowing faintly with flickering flame. Aya didn't hesitate. She started down the stairs, the walls breathing with heat and memory. Chrissy followed, tight behind her.

They entered a subterranean chamber — carved from volcanic stone, smooth and circular. At its center sat a pedestal, and atop it…

The Final Seal.

It wasn't just an object.

It was a burning emblem. Floating, suspended in the air. A ring of flame encasing a symbol Aya had never seen before — a fusion of all the Holloway sigils into something new. Something primal.

The third key glowed through its silk wrapping.

Chrissy touched Aya's arm. "This is it."

Aya nodded. "No turning back."

She stepped toward the seal — but the flames surged.

The whispers turned to screams.

From the shadows behind the flames, something massive stepped out.

It wasn't a person.

It wasn't even human.

It was the Curse made flesh — a creature stitched from ash and bone, its eyes hollow pits of fire. Every movement echoed with a thousand deaths.

"You are the final Holloway," it growled. "Break the seal, and you break the world. We are your legacy."

Aya gritted her teeth. "Then I reject it."

She pulled all three keys.

The curse lunged.

Chrissy screamed.

But Aya held her ground. The keys spun in her hands — faster and faster, glowing white, then gold, then silver — then something brighter than light. A blinding pulse erupted from the pedestal, throwing the curse back against the stone wall.

The Final Seal shattered.

And the world shifted.

Time cracked.

Reality wavered.

And Aya… fell.

[End of Chapter 35.]

CHAPTER THIRTY-SIX

Blood and Ashes

Aya hit the ground hard—but it wasn't stone.

It was grass.

Green, soft, living.

Birdsong filled the air. Sunlight filtered through a canopy of trees that were full and thriving. The forest was alive.

And so was she.

Her clothes were scorched. Her palms bled from gripping the keys. But she was breathing. Blinking. Whole.

Chrissy landed beside her moments later with a painful grunt, rolling to her side. "Where the hell…?"

Aya sat up slowly.

They were no longer beneath Ashenridge Forest. They were in a version of it before the fire. The trees were untouched, the soil rich, the air buzzing with insects and possibility.

"This is the past," Chrissy whispered. "This is what it used to be."

Aya turned toward a low humming sound.

There, standing under a massive oak, was the same ghostly woman from before—now fully solid. Warm. Human. She wore a faded red dress and a golden ring identical to Aya's.

"My name was Elira Holloway," she said softly. "The first."

Aya's breath caught in her throat. "You created the seal."

"I created the curse," Elira corrected. "And now you've brought me back to the moment it began."

The forest shimmered around them—like reality was waiting.

"You have a choice," Elira said, stepping closer. "You can relive my mistake. Or rewrite it."

Aya stood, keys still warm in her hand. She looked around—at the thriving woods, the peace, the promise.

Then at Chrissy.

"We're not the same," Aya said. "We're not bound by blood. We're bound by purpose."

She stepped into the clearing, feeling the ground pulse beneath her feet. The keys lifted on their own, spinning above her head, drawing fire and wind and memory from every direction.

Elira smiled. "Then do it."

Aya released the keys.

They flew into the sky and exploded in light.

Blinding, burning, searing light.

The wind howled. The trees bent. The seal shattered—not in destruction, but in rebirth.

And then—silence.

The world pulsed once.

Twice.

Then settled.

Aya blinked again.

She stood at the edge of Holloway's ruins—but they weren't ruins anymore. They were rebuilt. Restored. The ash was gone. The forest stood tall, reborn from centuries of pain.

The curse... was gone.

Chrissy laughed. A real one. "You did it."

"We did it," Aya said.

They stood together, the past behind them, the future unwritten.

Aya could still feel the scars. But they didn't burn anymore.

They reminded her of what she'd overcome—and what she could protect.

For the first time in generations, the Holloway name meant something new. Hope.

[THE END]

COPYRIGHT PAGE

BLOODLINE BOUND

© 2025 Sha'Ron Robertson
All rights reserved.

ISBN (Paperback): 979-8-9941814-3-0
Cover and interior design by Sha'Ron Robertson
Published by **Ember & Ink Publishing**

For more information, inquiries, or permissions, contact:
Ember & Ink Publishing
Chicago, Illinois

Printed in the United States of America
First Edition, 2025